THE

LADY GRACE
MYSTERIES

DECEPTION

Grace Cavendish

Patricia Finney is writing as Grace Cavendish

RED FOX

THE LADY GRACE MYSTERIES: DECEPTION
A RED FOX BOOK 978 1 862 30379 9

First published in Great Britain by Doubleday,
an imprint of Random House Children's Books
A Random House Group Company

Doubleday edition published 2004
Red Fox edition published 2007

1 3 5 7 9 10 8 6 4 2

Series created by Working Partners Ltd
Copyright © Working Partners Ltd, 2004

The right of Working Partners Ltd to be identified as the author
of this work has been asserted in accordance with the
Copyright, Designs and Patents Act 1988.

The Random House Group Limited makes every effort to ensure that the
papers used in its books are made from trees that have been legally sourced
from well-managed and credibly certified forests. Our paper procurement
policy can be found at: www.randomhouse.co.uk/paper.htm

Mixed Sources
Product group from well-managed
forests and other controlled sources
www.fsc.org Cert no. TT-COC-2139
© 1996 Forest Stewardship Council
FSC

Set in Bembo by Palimpsest Book Production Limited, Grangemouth, Stirlingshire

Red Fox Books are published by Random House Children's Books,
61–63 Uxbridge Road, London W5 5SA

www.kidsatrandomhouse.co.uk
www.rbooks.co.uk

Addresses for companies within The Random House Group Limited
can be found at: www.randomhouse.co.uk/offices.htm

THE RANDOM HOUSE GROUP Limited Reg. No. 954009

A CIP catalogue record for this book is available from the British Library.

Printed and bound in Great Britain by CPI Bookmarque,
Croydon, CR0 4TD

With grateful thanks to Dickie and Chic
and all the helpful staff at the
Tower of London

For mine own Eyes and None Other!

The Daybooke of my Lady Grace
Cavendish, Maid of Honour to
Her Gracious Majesty
Queen Elizabeth I of that name

At Her Majesty's Palace of
Whitehall, Westminster

The Twenty-third Day of November, in the Year of Our Lord 1569

The Queen's Presence Chamber – after breakfast

I have a new daybooke and I am so excited to begin writing in it! I am determined to keep this book neat and tidy with my best lettering throughout – and not make it look as if a drunken spider has crawled over it.

I am seated on a cushion with the other Maids of Honour in the Queen's Presence Chamber awaiting Her Majesty's arrival. She is busy with matters of state. We have a huge fire, for it has been mightily cold this last week. Indeed, the river Thames itself has frozen! The ice is thick enough to walk on and everyone is talking about the Frost Fair that has been set up on the frozen water near the landing steps to the Inns of Court. It is so exciting! We hope to visit today, when Her

Majesty has finally finished with boring state business.

Outside, the ice and frost look very inviting, but inside it is gloomy and we have much need of candles. The other Maids are working at their embroidery and Mrs Champernowne, Mistress of the Maids, is scowling at me for not doing the same. She looks ready to pounce the instant I make the tiniest ink blot upon my kirtle. But she dare not chide me too much, as Her Majesty herself gave me this daybooke and my fine quills and ink bottle. Ha, ha, Mrs Champernowne!

The Queen is my favourite person in the whole world. She has taken me under her wing and often shows me great kindness, because—

Hell's teeth! I have nearly spoiled my book already. I had to duck from a flying cushion. It would seem that the matters of state did not go well, for the Queen has just burst in and is now roaring round the chamber like a baited bear.

Lord-a-mercy, I'm not sure I should

compare Her Majesty to a bear – baited or otherwise. However, this daybooke is for my eyes alone, so I don't think I shall have my head cut off! Besides, as I was about to write before the cushion interrupted me, I am a favourite with Her Majesty the Queen (except when she throws things). She has never forgotten that my dear mother, God rest her soul, died saving her life last year. My mother was Her Majesty's close companion, and the Queen was almost as sad as I was when she died. So she made me a Maid of Honour, though I was only twelve, and vowed to protect me always. And now I am also Her Majesty's secret Lady Pursuivant. If she should cut off my head, who would then pursue all wrongdoers who trouble the Queen's peace?

Oh, dear, Her Majesty is glaring our way. I shall put my daybooke away for a while before some accident befalls it.

Later this Day, still in the Queen's Presence Chamber

The royal storm has now abated – but it was most exciting while it lasted.

Her Majesty paced up and down, flapping a letter she'd just received, looking as if she would breathe fire on the poor messenger, who cowered in the doorway waiting for an answer.

'What do you think is in that letter?' Lady Sarah whispered.

'Mayhap there is another problem with the new coin Her Majesty is having minted,' Mary Shelton suggested as she laid down the bonnet she is embroidering for her new niece.

'What problems are those?' asked Lady Jane, wide-eyed.

I was surprised that Lady Jane could have missed the tantrums and countless changes of mind the Queen had had. It had taken Her Majesty months to choose a design that pleased her. Mr Anthony, her engraver, was up to the palace with new designs almost every day.

We were all greatly relieved when Her Majesty finally declared that the pattern of a griffin rampant would adorn the new, pure silver coin. Her Majesty told me once that she thinks the griffin to be the epitome of nobility, with its head of an eagle and its body of a lion. I think it looks a bit ugly, but I wouldn't tell the Queen!

Lady Sarah sniffed and shook her coppery locks. 'Your ears are stoppered unless people are talking about you,' she told Lady Jane.

There is not much love lost between Lady Sarah Bartelmy and Lady Jane Coningsby. They each consider themselves the most beautiful of the Maids, and it leads to a good deal of bickering. They both want to make good marriages, and they see themselves as rivals for the favours of the young gentlemen of the Court. I myself have no time for such silliness.

'How dare you! You foolish flax-wench!' spluttered Lady Jane.

'But I thought the problems with the coin had all been settled,' said Penelope Knollys.

'Silence!' bellowed the Queen from the other end of the chamber. 'May I not have a second's peace to think?' and she looked about her for another missile to throw.

We ducked our heads down and busied ourselves with our work.

As there was nothing within reach, the Queen went on with her pacing. She always looks particularly impressive when she's angry, with her flame-red hair and her flashing eyes. Her white silk gown swished as she marched and her pearl ropes rattled with every step. Even the gold embroidery on her gown seemed to flash in temper.

She wrestled with the letter as if about to tear it into shreds. 'I cannot believe it,' she said through clenched teeth. 'Finally, all is well with the design of my new coin, and now Sir Edward Latimer dares to write me from the Royal Mint that there is not enough silver there to mint it! By Heaven, they shall find silver quick enough when they hear of my wrath!'

There was a whimper from the doorway and I thought the messenger was going to faint.

'Get you to Sir Edward with all haste,' the Queen bellowed at him, 'and tell him that he shall sort this business immediately or I shall remove him from the post of Mint Warden.'

The messenger bowed his way out, and we heard him scuttling down the corridor.

'He runs as if Cerberus himself were snapping at his heels with all three heads at once,' I whispered to Mary. I like that expression. I heard Her Majesty say it once and I have been determined to use it ever since.

Mary was looking puzzled. 'Who is Cerberus?' she hissed.

'The mythological dog who guarded the gate of Hades,' I told her, feeling very learned, though I confess I had to ask who he was when first I heard his name!

The Queen hurled the letter down and tried to grind it to a pulp under her heel. Then she stomped to the window and stared out.

'I fancy we shan't be going to the Frost Fair,' muttered Carmina Willoughby.

'I think you're right,' agreed Mary Shelton, jabbing her needle into the bonnet and pricking her finger. She sucked at it miserably.

I was feeling miserable too – and I still am. I've been looking forward to the Frost Fair, of course, but most of all I've been longing to go on the ice again. Just last week, a young Dutch nobleman introduced us all to a new sport. It's called skating. We were tutored on the frozen lake in the park of St James and now it has become very fashionable at Court. It seems the Hollanders do it every winter on their frozen waterways.

When I first saw the strange flat undershoes with a sharp length of bone beneath them, I wondered how I'd ever stay upright. I feared I would be as good on the ice as I am on a horse – which is to say, very bad! But when the skates were tied firmly to my boots with leather straps I found to my amazement that I had a talent for it. The funniest thing was that Lady Jane, who was desperate to impress the young – and unmarried – Dutch nobleman, couldn't skate at all. At other times, my haughty lady is very inclined to look down her nose at me – but on the ice she found herself mostly looking up!

'I really don't think you should upset your-selves about a mere Frost Fair,' said Lady Jane in her superior way.

'But it would have been such fun!' exclaimed Penelope.

'It wouldn't have been much fun for me,' sniffed Lady Sarah.

I was surprised at this. I could understand Lady Jane not wanting to make a fool of herself on the ice again, but I had thought Lady Sarah would be happy to go. Her skating wasn't bad and she impressed enough of the young courtiers last time to satisfy her vanity. That pleased her on two accounts. She loves to impress young men and she loves to look better than Lady Jane. So what could be the problem?

'How can I possibly go when I have not received the new gown I was promised?' Lady Sarah wailed – very quietly so that the Queen wouldn't hear her.

By my soul! I thought. How could I have forgotten about the New Gown? She has been going on about it for days and we all know the story by heart. But that did not deter Lady Sarah from boring us again.

'It is so vexing. My Uncle Richard has gone back on his word!' she moaned. 'When he made so much money from that investment, he said' – and here she looked round to make sure we were all paying attention – '"What better way to use my riches than to adorn a beautiful niece in fine raiment?"' The beautiful niece smiled sweetly at us. 'His words, not mine.'

I caught Mary Shelton's eye and pretended I was going to be sick, which made her laugh. Sarah's complaints hold no sway with Mary and me. She has so many clothes I'm surprised that any of us can move in our bedchamber for trunks and presses.

''Tis such a pity that there was a robbery at his London house, and he says he cannot now afford it,' said Carmina solemnly, although her eyes were dancing with mirth.

'But indeed he can!' chanted Mary Shelton, imitating Lady Sarah. 'He still has great riches remaining and thus can easily pay for one new gown.'

We all tittered at that – except for Lady Sarah, who had already launched into a long complaint about how her uncle certainly had enough money but was just sulking about the robbery.

Will she ever stop mewling on about it? Perhaps I shall write to her Uncle Richard myself, and plead with him to buy her the wretched gown before we all go deaf.

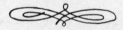

Later this Day – my own bedchamber

I am trying to write amid the excited shrieking of Lady Sarah and Mary Shelton. We are to go to the Frost Fair after all! And it is thanks to Lady Sarah's moans, which had become louder and louder as she told her tale. With a furious look, Her Majesty suddenly reached for a painted glass bowl and turned towards us. Lady Sarah couldn't see this, as she was facing the fire, or she would certainly have held her peace. With a roar, the Queen threw the bowl and it smashed on the floor, just behind Lady Sarah. I would have laughed at the expression on Sarah's face if I hadn't been so scared myself!

'Out of my sight, my whingeing lady!' yelled Her Majesty, striding towards her like a great white galleon. 'I am sick of the sound of your voice!'

Blushing crimson, Lady Sarah bundled up her embroidery and crept out. The rest of us sat, not daring to move a muscle, and hoping not to be the next target.

But Her Majesty was under full sail, with all guns blazing. 'And the rest of you!' she bellowed.

We jumped to our feet and curtsied hurriedly.

'I will not be surrounded by prating fools! I care not where you go, but begone before I—'

We didn't wait to find out what Her Majesty had in mind. As Mary pulled the chamber door shut behind us, we heard the sound of a royal shoe clattering against the wood.

'That was a narrow escape!' I panted, as we paused for breath in the Privy Gallery. We couldn't hear the sounds of the Queen's tirade any more and decided we were probably safe.

'I have never been more frightened in my whole life!' declared Lady Sarah. Of course that was nonsense, but two young gentlemen had just stopped to find out what was amiss — or rather to admire Sarah's bosom, which was heaving dramatically for them.

'What are we going to do now?' asked Mary despondently. 'We must avoid Her Majesty at all costs.'

'All I want to do is get on my skates and go to the Frost Fair,' sighed Penelope.

'Well, we could!' I declared.

They all looked at me, aghast.

'But the Queen . . .' began Mary, glancing round anxiously as if Her Majesty were hanging from the ceiling, ready to drop onto her head.

'The Queen said she didn't care where we went,' I pointed out, 'so she won't care if we go to the Frost Fair, will she?'

And now Lady Sarah, Mary Shelton and I are in the bedchamber we share, making ready to go. Sometimes I long for a chamber of my own, but that would be unheard of. In truth Mary and I get along well, and even Lady Sarah is not too bad, I suppose – when she is not whining on about gowns, or her spots.

I have been ready for an age in my thickest and oldest green woollen kirtle – it is fast becoming too short for me and so it is easier to skate in. I have my fur-lined cloak and skates by my side.

After much deliberation, Lady Sarah has decided on a gown to wear. She says it will 'just about do', for she has had it at least a month and considers it rather old. She is now fussing over her face mask. She cannot find it anywhere. If she does not wear it, the cold will ruin her delicate complexion, she keeps telling us. I would have thought her face already well-covered — she puts enough potions on it. But Mrs Champernowne soon jumps on us if we don't wear our masks to protect our skin when we go out in winter time.

If it was me I'd be glad I had lost it. Masks are the silliest idea I can think of. Because they can only be held in place by a button that is grasped with the teeth, they become uncomfortable after a while. And, worst of all, you cannot easily talk while wearing one.

We will certainly be a big party. When the young gentlemen of the Court heard that Lady Jane and Lady Sarah would be going, they fell over each other in their offers to attend us Maids of Honour. And when the Ladies-in-Waiting heard that the young gentlemen would be attending, they too were most eager to join the party. At this rate the whole palace will be empty!

Lady Sarah is still hunting for her cursed mask. Perchance I should offer her mine and be done with it.

Heaven be praised! All is sorted: 'Take my mask,' I said to Lady Sarah, holding it out. 'I don't need it.'

'That's true,' Lady Sarah replied, almost snatching it from me. 'You do not have such fine skin as I do.' She held it against her cloak. 'It is not a good match, but better than nothing, I suppose.'

Ungrateful girl!

But never mind. I have now escaped wearing the mask: Mrs Champernowne can say nothing against such an act of mercy – and we will have peace at last from my lady's moans.

It is time to hide my daybooke away and go.

Two hours after noon

Having come back to my chamber, thrown my cloak down, been moaned at by Mrs Champernowne, picked the cloak up again and folded it, I am at last left alone to write.

I need to see the Queen urgently, but she is closeted with Sir William Cecil on matters of state and will not be disturbed at least until sunset. So I will take the opportunity to write all about the fair – and the mystery I have uncovered. There has been a— No, I must set this out as it happened, or I may miss out something important.

We all set off, chattering, through the palace, with Mrs Champernowne calling dire warnings after us. 'Don't go skating off on your own, look you!' she told us. 'There'll be no more ice frolics for those who behave in an unseemly way today.'

I'm sure she must have had her beady eyes on me as she said it.

We came out of the palace and onto Privy Bridge. Strange that it is called a bridge, as it is really just a landing stage for Whitehall. Everyone knows there is only one bridge across the Thames, and that is London Bridge. One of the Queen's boatmen told me he blames London Bridge for the Thames being frozen. He explained that ice blocks from upriver floated down and stuck against its close arches and gradually the water upstream froze over. God bless London Bridge, I say!

All along the bank were more great blocks of ice that must have been caught there as the river froze. If I half closed my eyes I could imagine they were white mountains, like the ones I've seen in paintings from foreign lands.

Someone had cut steps through the blocks onto the flatter ice further out on the river. We made our way down, then sat on our cloaks to strap on our skates. We could see the Frost Fair in the distance and many people making their way to it.

'Look at us!' I called to Mary Shelton, as I pushed off across the ice. 'We're on the Thames without a boat!'

'I don't like the thought of all that freezing water beneath us,' Mary replied, looking down and wobbling a little.

'Have no fear, my lady!' smiled Sir Peter Howlett, one of our escorts. He circled us and raised his hat with a flourish. 'The ice is a foot thick at the very least.'

'And people are walking along it as if it's just another street,' I reassured her.

'Don't tarry,' cried Penelope, as she glided expertly past us. 'We want to get to the fair!'

I followed. Skating is a wonderful feeling. To think that a little bit of bone strapped to a piece of wood can take you skimming across the ice as fast as a galloping horse!

Some of the gentlemen decided to have a race, weaving in and out of the crowds. Sir Peter won and scratched his name in the ice with his dagger. Then he added the names of his 'fair companions'. He was eager to point out that he had carved Lady Sarah's closest to his. Lady Sarah tried to pretend she didn't care, but I could see she was pleased.

I had a sneaking look back at Lady Jane to see how she was faring. She had lost her mask and was becoming quite red in the face as she desperately tried to stay upright. My fine lady would have been much better fluttering her eyelashes at the very start and gaining a gentleman's arm to lean on. Heavens! To think I know more of flirting on ice than Lady Jane! Not that I would ever put it into practice.

As we drew near the fair, we could hear the hubbub and see the bright colours of the tents and stalls. I couldn't wait to have a closer look.

But just then, Mary Shelton skidded up to me, grabbed hold of my arm and turned us both in circles. 'For the love of God, Grace,' she giggled, 'help me. I want to go to the Frost Fair but my skates have other ideas!'

A couple of dirty-faced urchins raced past pulling a sled behind them. A merchant and his wife sat uncomfortably upon it. Carmina looked longingly at the sled.

'Want a ride, ladies?' called one of the urchins. 'Only tuppence to the fair. We'll come back for you.' But at that moment the sled hit a bump and deposited the merchant and his wife on the ice. The urchins left in a hurry . . .

'I think I'm safer with you, Grace,' said Mary as she wobbled along.

At last, after a lot of giggling and slipping about, we all arrived at the Frost Fair. I was surprised at how big it was. It put me in mind of the great St Bartholomew's Fair at Fynnesbury Field.

I was itching to explore – but I knew I would be in terrible disgrace if I skated off unattended. Even though Mrs Champernowne had not come with us, she would hear of it somehow. Nothing escapes her flapping ears.

Our great party skated along together, enjoying the fair. There were bright tents all over the ice, selling everything from puppets to pasties.

'Where have all these stalls come from?' exclaimed Carmina. 'It looks as if all the market traders in London are here.'

'And all the Londoners too, I'd wager,' added Penelope.

'Look yonder!' gasped Mary. 'A whole ox is being roasted over by the bank. It's a wonder the ice does not melt!'

In some places, the ice was almost invisible from the rubbish and dung that covered it. I was pleased that I'd worn my shortest kirtle to avoid trailing it in the mess.

Lady Jane had at last found herself a prop. Robert Neale was gallantly staggering about with her. But she didn't seem much gratified – mayhap because there was no chance of making Lady Sarah jealous with such an escort. He is rather fat and seems always to smell of boiled cabbage.

It didn't take long for the young gentlemen to be drawn towards a large, noisy tent with a flagon of ale painted on its side. I could see a lot of red-faced men around it – and I don't think it was just the cold that made their cheeks glow. I wondered how much of an escort our young gentlemen would be to us after they had quaffed a few flagons of the 'Dragon's Milk' and 'Mad Dog' ales that were being offered with great hearty shouts. I noticed that Lady Jane's escort was gallant enough not to leave her side, however; then I realized why. Her fingers were digging into his sleeve like the talons of a hawk into its prey.

I led the rest of the party to a low trestle where breads and savouries were on display. We paid our pennies and fell upon the saffron cakes, for the exercise and cold had made us famished.

'Now come and look at the sweets,' said Lady Sarah, dragging us over to a booth full of gingerbreads, candies and frosted fruits.

The stallholder was a cheery man. 'Buy while you can, fair ladies,' he said, with an attempt at a courtly bow. 'I am only here while my master Mr Frost allows me. Soon Mr Thaw will come along, and I have the sinking feeling that I shall have to pack up my wares and swim!'

'Then we must make haste,' I smiled. I liked his clever words, and bought a dozen ribbon-shaped sweets and some sugared plums, even though he had put up his prices like all the other sellers at the Frost Fair. I have a great sweet tooth and I knew that Ellie, who is always hungry, would enjoy sharing them. I thought about my two best friends, working hard at the palace – Ellie in the laundry and Masou in Will Somers's acrobatic troupe. It makes me sad that Ellie and Masou and I cannot be friends openly because of the difference in our stations. The Queen knows all about it, of course, but would never mention it. My daybooke is the only place I can talk of our friendship.

As we left the stall, we heard a sudden peal of bells from the church on Lambeth bank. It meant the Queen was coming! The bells always ring whenever she takes to the river.

A band of men hurried by with brooms and shovels, pushing aside the rubbish and horse dung that littered the ice – and anyone who got in their way. Then there came a great fanfare from the direction of Whitehall.

The crowds parted as heralds in red coats marched along, blowing on their trumpets. And following them was the Queen, her guard and a whole retinue of courtiers. Her Majesty had changed her mind about the Frost Fair. I hoped she'd changed her temper too or we'd all be in trouble!

The young gentlemen left the beer tent, anxiously wiping their mouths. Some were a little unsteady on their skates. Robert Neale somehow managed to shake off Lady Jane and hurried away towards the Queen. He needs to stay in Her Majesty's favour. Being only a second son and having no fortune, he wants a good position at Court.

Lady Jane flapped about, desperate to keep up with us as we scurried towards the north bank to join the royal party. But in the hustle and bustle she was knocked off balance. She tried to save herself, but her arm-waving just sent her in the wrong direction and she hurtled away towards the south bank, flailing like a windmill and scattering people as she went. She sped past Lady Sarah who, instead of putting out a helping hand, carefully lifted her skirts out of the way.

As Lady Jane approached the bank she crashed though the branches of a weeping willow and disappeared. Mary and I couldn't help giggling. It was such a funny sight.

But then Lady Jane let out a bloodcurdling scream. Concerned now, I skated over, the other Maids of Honour following.

'I wonder what's happened this time,' sighed Lady Sarah as we struggled together through the branches. 'She is so dramatic.' Then she stopped, open-mouthed.

Lady Jane was clinging to the side of a waterman's rowing boat that was frozen in the ice. Inside the boat was a dead body.

Its face was deathly white and its lips grey. It had been blindfolded.

Lady Sarah looked as if she was going to be sick and Carmina and Penelope had gone very pale. Lady Jane whimpered feebly as Mary Shelton helped her to her feet and away from the horrible sight.

I could hear voices behind me. A few of the fair-goers had begun to gather.

'What's all the commotion?'

'Some fellow's dead in his boat!'

'Died of cold, did he?'

But I could see that this was no natural death. I tried to get closer for a better look. Before I could discover any more, however, some of the Queen's Guard pushed through the crowd with their leader, Mr Christopher Hatton.

As soon as Mr Hatton saw the body he started issuing orders. 'Escort these ladies to

Her Majesty,' he told his men. 'I will go ahead and acquaint her of the facts.' He threw some money to a man nearby. 'You stay here and guard the body until the undertaker's labourers arrive. Do a good job and you shall be further rewarded.'

The man touched his cap and stood by the boat with his arms folded, looking very important.

Mr Hatton hurried off to the Queen. One of his men took Lady Jane firmly by the arm and led her away. The Maids of Honour followed. I didn't want to leave the scene – I was desperate to learn what had happened to the poor man in the boat. It was such a mystery and just such an event as a Lady Pursuivant should investigate. But there was nothing I could do – at least, nothing yet. Reluctantly I skated after the other Maids.

In the distance, I could see that a huge crowd had gathered to watch the Queen's party as it made its way across the cleared ice towards the stalls of the Frost Fair. There was much cheering, and shouts of 'God Bless Your Majesty!'

As we reached the edge of the crowd, the people jostled and didn't seem very keen to let us through, until they saw the Gentlemen of the Guard with their long, fierce-looking halberds.

Mr Hatton bowed low in front of Her Majesty and we all curtsied.

'What took you so hurriedly from my side, Mr Hatton?' Her Majesty asked, removing her mask to stare at us all sternly. 'Surely it was not just to round up my twittering Maids of Honour like a sheepdog?'

The Queen's temper did not seem much improved. We all tried to look demure and obedient as Mr Hatton quickly told her about the body in the boat.

'May God have mercy on his soul,' said the Queen. 'I leave the arrangements in your hands, Mr Hatton.' Then she looked irritably at Lady Jane, who was casting her eyes at all the young gentlemen and moaning faintly. 'I believe Lady Jane would be better served if she were to return to the palace,' she said.

Several young men stepped forward to offer

their arm. But to Lady Jane's obvious dismay, and Lady Sarah's obvious delight, Mrs Champernowne suddenly appeared at her side and marched, or rather, *slid* her off towards Privy Bridge.

When they were gone, the Queen suddenly smiled and held out her hand to a gentleman at her side. I recognized him immediately. He was Sir Edward Latimer, her Mint Warden, and the cause of the Queen's furious cushion-throwing earlier.

'You will lend me your arm, Sir Edward, and escort me over the ice,' she commanded. 'I wish to see this Frost Fair and you have now the opportunity to remedy the displeasure of your Queen. I have not yet forgiven you for the delay with my new coin.'

Sir Edward is handsome and always finely dressed. He is tall and dark-haired, and today he wore a green velvet suit the exact same colour as his glittering eyes – as Lady Jane was quick to notice. He drew a lot of attention from the ladies. But he had eyes only for the Queen. Every time she spoke to him, he preened like one of the peacocks in the grounds of Whitehall. He must be a man of wealth for he always has his own servants with him – three young pages and a large body-guard.

I know that the other Maids of Honour are greatly impressed with Sir Edward, but I'm not. And his behaviour today didn't help. Whenever the corpse was mentioned, he gasped like a girl and pressed an embroidered handkerchief to his mouth – and he hadn't even seen the body! I am quite surprised that such a milk-livered dandy should be entrusted with the Royal Mint.

But then Sir Edward's supporter at Court is Sir Thomas Gresham, Her Majesty's Chief Financier. It was Sir Thomas who helped the Queen restore our coinage after her own father, Henry VIII, had debased it so much that it was almost worthless. The debased coins were made of a cheap mixture of copper and a tiny amount of silver. The copper made the silver go further, and the coins cheaper to produce, but it soon made them worthless too. What silver there was quickly rubbed away on the prominent bits of the coin – like King Henry's nose. I have heard that some called him Coppernose because of this – behind his back, of course, for they wished to keep their heads! And Sir Thomas helped remedy all this, so he is a clever man and would surely not offer a fool his support.

Perhaps I've been too hard on Sir Edward. It must be a complicated job being in charge of all the coinage of the realm – especially when the Queen holds up the plans and then expects her Mint Warden to produce silver for making new coins out of thin air.

If nothing else, Sir Edward was certainly having a good effect on Her Majesty's temper. He was paying her endless compliments – and there is nothing the Queen likes better from a handsome gentleman. She was all smiles now!

'I fear that the ice itself may melt in the glow of Your Majesty's presence,' Sir Edward was saying.

While the other Maids of Honour stared goggle-eyed at the glamorous Sir Edward, I was desperate to get back to the body in the boat and have another look before it was taken to a coroner. I wondered if I could sneak off while Sir Edward was making his pretty speeches to the Queen. But Her Majesty was in such a good mood now that she wanted us to enjoy the fair with her. She thought it would be great sport to watch the Maids of Honour play skittles and she had spotted a skittle alley among the stalls. As we made our way towards it I could hear Sir Edward comparing the Queen with everything in sight:

'The finest of frost patterns cannot compete with Your Grace's beauty,' and 'I see that Helios himself dare not show his face while our Royal Sun is shining upon us.'

Hell's teeth! Why does Her Majesty like all that silliness? I wondered what would happen if Sir Edward got carried away and compared her to the roasting ox.

However, everyone else seemed mightily impressed with his words, especially the Queen, who looked as if she wouldn't have cared now if he produced coins made of cowpats.

Skittles on skates is not easy! The Queen soon tired of our antics, although she did laugh heartily when Carmina tripped and slid all the way up the skittle alley. All the skittles went flying – and she was still holding the ball.

The Queen's eye was next caught by an archery contest near the south bank, and the whole party swept off to watch.

Our route took us past the boat containing the blindfolded corpse and I seized the opportunity to slip to the back of the party in hopes of getting a closer look. I could see that the undertaker's labourers were arriving with a sled. I decided I had to get there without delay or the body would be gone!

I quickly skated over to the boat while Sir Edward was jabbering on about Her Majesty being more slender and graceful than the finest bow in England.

The man guarding the body was talking with some bystanders while the undertaker's men examined his charge. The bystanders touched their caps and moved apart to let me through.

'Do you know who it is then?' one of them asked the guard.

'Ay,' nodded the guard importantly. ''Tis a waterman from Westminster way, name of Will Stubbs.'

'I know of him,' gasped a woman, putting her hands to her head. 'They say he went missing, just before the ice set. Oh, his poor wife.'

One of the undertaker's men had started to remove the blindfold from the dead man. He uttered an oath of surprise as the cloth came away to reveal two silver coins, one placed over each eye. 'Look at these!' he said to the other labourer, picking them up and peering at them closely. 'I've never seen coins like this.'

'Nor I,' said his friend, 'but they've got Her Majesty's head on them, right enough.'

I could feel my heart pounding in my chest – the mystery was deepening. I knew I had to get a look at those coins. 'Let me see,' I said quickly.

The men didn't move.

'Those coins have been bound to a dead man's eyes,' said the man holding the coins. 'Have you no fear of his spirit, my lady?'

'Indeed not,' I replied firmly. 'What can a dead man do? It is the one who has done this foul deed that we should fear.'

There was a gasp at my bold words, but still the man did not hand the coins to me.

I drew myself up and looked him square in the eye. 'Enough of this shilly-shallying!' I said. 'Give me the coins.' Shilly-shallying is one of Her Majesty's favourite expressions and I was trying to sound like her as I said it.

The labourer who had the coins held them out sheepishly on his palm.

I took them from him, and as I examined them, my stomach lurched in surprise. They had the Queen's head on one side and the griffin rampant on the other – exactly the design that the Queen had finally chosen for her new coin. But it was impossible! I had seen drawings of them at the palace, but none had been minted yet.

I realized that everyone was watching me. 'The Queen will need to see these,' I said in my most imperious voice, just in case someone tried to argue. 'I will take them to her directly.'

The undertaker's labourers shrugged and lifted Will Stubbs's body onto their sled.

'We better take him to the coroner in Southwark,' said one.

'We're near the south bank, I grant you,' grunted the other, 'but the City's just yonder. Old Dr Folgate keeps a good fire. We could warm ourselves there for a bit.'

'Don't be a noddlehead!' the first one answered. 'He's got to go to the coroner in charge of where he's been found.'

'Don't you call me a noddlehead!' said his friend. 'There isn't a coroner for the river, unless it be old Father Thames, and we don't know where he keeps court!'

As they argued, I suddenly had an idea. 'Pray bear him to Dr Cavendish at Whitehall Palace,' I instructed them. 'He is the Queen's Coroner, and the nearest.' I didn't tell the men that he is also my uncle and that if there was foul play afoot regarding the Queen's new coin, then Her Majesty might want me, her secret Lady Pursuivant, to investigate.

With the coins safely in the pocket of my kirtle, I hurried to catch up with the Royal Party. I could not wait for the chance to tell Her Majesty what I had found out.

But it was impossible to get past the wretched Sir Edward – a plague on him! Her Majesty glowered at me every time I tried to interrupt his flatteries and speak with her.

Now we are back at Whitehall and I have written pages and pages in my daybooke – but still I have not spoken to Her Majesty. I think I am going to burst!

Later this Day – five of the clock just striking

At last I have been able to tell the Queen about the coins. And in doing so, I have uncovered yet more of this mystery!

When word went out that the Queen had left her Presence Chamber, I hurried over to the busy Great Hall, with the coins in my pocket, and jostled my way towards her through the crowd.

'Forgive me, Your Majesty . . .' I said, and curtsied so hurriedly that she nearly fell over me. 'I am in haste as I need to speak to you in private, and most urgently.'

'Not now, Grace,' answered the Queen, with a sigh. 'Unfortunately, I have many papers still to sign and Secretary Cecil is most anxious for me to attend to them.'

I knew I had to make her understand how important this was, but I had to speak in code for fear of anyone overhearing. 'If it please Your Majesty, two of your new *silver griffins* have escaped.'

The Queen looked at me. Her expression did not change but I could see from her eyes that she understood. She shooed everyone away, then led me to her private Withdrawing Chamber and closed the door.

'Well?' she asked curiously. 'What is this about my new coins, Grace?'

I took the two coins from my pocket and held them out. 'You will recall the corpse found in the boat at the Frost Fair, Your Majesty,' I said. 'These were bound to the poor man's eyes with a blindfold. I believe they are two of your new coins.'

The Queen stared at the coins as if she could not believe her eyes. Then, without a word, she took a key from a chain round her neck, strode over to her desk and opened a small golden casket that lay there. Six shining silver coins lay within.

She scooped them up. 'How can this be?' she murmured, putting the six coins down on the desk and taking up the two from my hand. 'Mine are the only six to have been released from the Royal Mint. All the other newly minted coins are locked up at the Tower. Not one is supposed to be in circulation, and yet here are two, looking like my six in every way.'

She tossed the coins onto the desk with the others, then began pacing about the room in thought.

I stared at the small pile of coins and

suddenly noticed something. The six belonging to the Queen were shiny, as if they had been polished. But the remaining two were slightly different.

'Begging Your Majesty's pardon!' I exclaimed excitedly.

The Queen stopped and looked at me enquiringly.

'I believe that the two coins I brought to you are not exact copies of yours,' I explained.

I held up one of the Queen's coins against the two others. 'These two new ones are duller – I think they cannot be pure silver.'

Her Majesty looked closely at them. 'They must be counterfeit!' she hissed. 'This is even more serious!' Her shoulders slumped. She looked tired and careworn. 'Ah, Grace!' she said. 'I have worked ceaselessly to give our noble coinage back its true worth and now I fear it will come to nothing!' Then her eyes flashed and she lifted her head and became once again my bright, fiery Queen. 'This shall not be made public else the world will lose faith in our currency. The counterfeiters must be brought to justice – and swiftly. But who can they be?'

'Let me investigate,' I urged, 'if it pleases Your Majesty.'

The Queen smiled at me. 'My own Lady Pursuivant! It is a good idea, for nobody would suspect a Maid of Honour of investigating such a matter, and I do not wish the miscreant to know we have discovered the forgeries, for he might cover his tracks and we should never find the villain out. But you must make haste, Grace, for I have decreed that my new coins will be in circulation in less than a fortnight. You may have five days, but then I must hand the matter over to Sir Thomas Gresham for an official investigation. And mark, Grace, you must move secretly.'

'I have already had the corpse taken to my Uncle Cavendish,' I told her. 'I will learn more from him about the manner of death when I see him tomorrow – and the information will go no further.'

'I commend you for your quick thinking, Grace,' said the Queen.

This was great praise from Her Majesty and

I still feel a tingle of pride when I write of it.

The Queen studied the coins again. 'Although this matter must be kept in the utmost secrecy, I would have Sir Thomas look at these to confirm that they are indeed counterfeit. I trust him implicitly.'

Sir Thomas Gresham was summoned and arrived swiftly. He did not even deign to notice my presence.

Her Majesty handed him the two coins and told him how they'd been found. I saw his face grow pale as he examined the coins and compared them with the ones from the casket.

Then he gave me a haughty look. 'I would rather not speak in front of a Maid of Honour, My Liege,' he said. 'She is very young and likely to have a prattling tongue.'

I bristled at this, but the Queen leaped to my defence. 'It was Lady Grace Cavendish who brought this matter to our attention,' she said coldly. 'We trust her discretion absolutely and know her to be a true subject. We hope we may know the same of you!'

Sir Thomas fell to his knees. 'Indeed, Your Majesty. I am ever your faithful servant.'

'Then get up, man, and look to these coins!' snapped the Queen.

Sir Thomas struggled to his feet. 'I regret, My Liege, that these two coins are indeed forgeries,' he told her, and I could hear the fear in his voice as he confirmed the bad news. 'They are excellently made and it is only the slight variance in colour that gives them away, but they are fakes nonetheless.' He turned the false coins over in his hand. 'I have seen counterfeit coins before where the villains used wax to make a mould of the originals. The results were very poor copies,' he told us. 'But the designs on these are so accurate and clear that I am sure they have been struck like genuine coins from the original engraving. Such work would have required expert moneyers, using proper trussels and piles. But where could they have got the dies from?'

My head reeled. For all I understood he could have been talking in a foreign tongue.

'It seems to me,' Sir Thomas went on, 'that another mint must have been set up in order to make these counterfeit coins. Let me hunt down the miscreants without delay, Your Majesty. We have worked too hard to restore your currency to let this happen.'

'You will do nothing,' barked the Queen, 'if you wish to keep your head upon your shoulders! I have ordered my own investigation. And I would have you tell no one of this matter. I do not wish the villains to know that we have discovered their felony lest they should instantly take steps to hide the evidence. Besides, since the fakes are so well made, I fear that someone close to the mint must be involved.'

'But should I not tell Sir Edward, Your Majesty?' asked Sir Thomas. 'As Mint Warden—'

'Not even he,' ordered the Queen. 'There have been delays enough and I do not wish him to be further distracted from his work. If the villains have not been discovered in five days, then I may call you to investigate, but until then, not a word.'

Sir Thomas bowed. 'As Your Majesty commands,' he said reluctantly.

As soon as Sir Thomas and I were dismissed, I fetched my daybooke and hastened to the Long Gallery to write everything down. I realize that I have very little idea about how a coin is made and I must find out more about minting. If I am to find this illegal mint I ought to know what I am searching for.

And I need to see Ellie and Masou. I have less than a week to solve this crime and I need the help of my friends, for they have been true accomplices to me in the past – and they love a mystery!

In my bedchamber, late, under many cloaks

Lady Sarah and Mary Shelton are already asleep so I shall not be disturbed, except by their snoring. But my candle is flickering and has not much life left in it and I have no other in my chamber. I must be brief.

I was about to leave the Long Gallery to

find Ellie and Masou when the shout went up for a game of Maw.

'You like this one, Grace,' called Mary, rattling the pot that already had some players' bets in. 'Come and join us. I'll deal you a hand of cards.'

She was right – I love trying to win as many tricks as possible and claiming the contents of the pot, but today I had to think of an excuse. 'I'm sorry but I can't. I must . . . er . . . have some laundry attended to.'

'Can you not leave it until tomorrow?' asked Carmina.

'It is an ink blot on a sleeve,' I said. 'And Mrs Champernowne will be chiding me till Christmas if she sees it.'

'You would not get ink blots on you at all if you didn't waste so much time scribbling in that silly book!' said Lady Jane with a superior air.

I wished I could have scribbled all over her silly face.

I picked up my daybooke and penner before I was too tempted and stalked off to find Ellie.

Sometimes I wish Whitehall were not so

large and sprawling, with so many rooms and separate buildings. It is a great journey to reach the laundry where Ellie works.

I could just make out Ellie through the hot, steamy air of the laundry, up to her skinny elbows in soapy water. Poor Ellie. I wish she didn't have to work so hard. She is small and thin and I wonder she can lift the heavy sheets from the copper.

I walked boldly up to her. 'Ellie, I want you to look at my sleeve,' I said aloud, then bent forward and whispered, 'I have a new mystery and I must tell you about it!'

Ellie's eyes lit up. Then she looked worried. 'I can't, Grace,' she whispered back. 'I have these sheets to rinse and drape on the bushes tonight so the frost can make 'em white.'

'I'll help you,' I replied. 'Get Masou and meet me in the laundry garden as soon as you can.'

I raced back up to my chamber and pulled on my gloves and two cloaks – mine and Mary Shelton's. I didn't think she'd mind. Then I remembered the sugared plums I'd bought for

Ellie. I stuffed them into a pocket and made my way quietly through the palace and at last out to the laundry garden. I must have walked ten miles tonight with all the to-ing and fro-ing.

It was bitterly cold outside. If anyone had seen me going out into the frosty night air they'd have sent me to bed convinced I was mad with fever. I peered through the dark towards the bushes where the laundry was usually spread to dry, wishing I'd thought to bring a light. Then out of nowhere a lantern appeared and, hovering next to it, a disembodied head!

It stared menacingly at me, wailing like a fiend from hell. For an instant I believed it to be a traitor's head from one of the pikes on London Bridge. I would have taken to my heels in terror if the head hadn't started grinning in a way I knew all too well.

'You can't fool me, Masou!' I exclaimed, pretending I wasn't scared at all. It was a good job he couldn't see me quaking.

Masou took the lantern from his face and

held it up with one hand as he made a flourishing bow with the other. In the flickering light I could see he was wrapped in a heavy wool blanket to keep out the cold. Masou must feel the cold more than us, because he comes from Africa which, he says, is very hot.

'And I know you're there, Ellie!' I laughed, as I heard giggling from behind a hedge.

Ellie appeared, dragging a big wicker basket full of wet sheets. She was shivering in her thin clothes so I put Mary's cloak over her shoulders.

'Your face was a picture, Grace!' she chuckled, gratefully snuggling into the warm cloak.

'Now tell us of this mystery,' demanded Masou eagerly.

'I'll tell you in a minute,' I said, as I rummaged in my pocket and held out the sweetmeats I'd brought for Ellie.

Ellie grinned with delight and popped a sugared plum into her mouth, but Masou snatched the rest from me and started juggling them skilfully with one hand. I knew we needn't fear that he would drop them – but Ellie shrieked and chased him round the hedges, trying to grab the plums. Laughing, Masou gave up and tossed the sweets to her one at a time. Ellie stuffed them quickly in her mouth before anything else could happen to them.

Then Masou helped Ellie to carry the basket over to the laundry hedges. 'Out with it, Grace,' he said. 'Tell us your story.'

'A corpse was discovered at the Frost Fair!' I told them, as we spread the sheets out.

'There was talk in the laundry that someone got froze in the ice,' mumbled Ellie as she swallowed the last plum.

'Where's the mystery in that?' asked Masou, looking puzzled. 'Many die of cold in the winter. And I shall be among their number if I do not seek the solace of a fire soon.'

I ignored him. 'This was no ordinary death,' I said, and I told them how the waterman, Will Stubbs, had been found in the boat. Ellie and Masou grew wide-eyed as I got to the bit about two of the Queen's new coins being bound to Will Stubbs's eyes – and how these coins had proved to be counterfeit. 'The Queen has given me just five days to solve the mystery of the counterfeiting,' I finished. 'So you see I need your help.'

'Ever at your service, my lady,' declared Masou with an elaborate bow.

I hate it when he reminds me of the gap between our stations in life and I made to give him a shove.

But he jumped nimbly out of the way. 'The Queen's Troupe is to perform at the fair tomorrow,' he said. 'Allah knows, I do not relish the notion and if Mr Somers thinks I am going to stand on my hands on the ice he can think again. However, if by some happy chance I have not frozen solid, I will mingle with the crowd afterwards and keep my ears open.'

'And I'll listen to all the talk in the laundry,' promised Ellie, picking up her empty basket.

'And I shall go to my uncle,' I said. 'He may have discovered something important about the body.'

We agreed to meet up again as soon as we had any news to share.

Now I must finish, as my candle is spluttering.

The Twenty-fourth Day of November, in the Year of Our Lord 1569

Sunrise

I am writing by the first light of day. I am in my chamber and although Mary Shelton and Lady Sarah have not yet stirred, I have been up for more than an hour. My writing is rather wobbly as my fingers are freezing and may drop off at any moment. No one has been in yet to rekindle the fire.

As soon as I awoke this morning, I arose, hastily put on my kirtle, shirt and my warmest gown over my nightshift, and went to see my uncle in his chambers. Perhaps he would be able to throw some light on my mystery.

I had trouble waking him. I knocked on his door until my knuckles were sore before he appeared. When I saw him my heart sank. It was clear he had drunk too much mead at table the night before, and his eyes were bleary and bloodshot. I followed him into his living chamber. It was strewn with papers and forgotten meals and it stank! I wanted to open a window. My Uncle Cavendish is a fine doctor, but the mead and wine dull his wits.

'What's amiss, Grace?' he slurred. 'Why d'you call on me so early? Are you ill?'

He looked concerned. He is very fond of me and I of him, but I cannot confide in him about my investigations as he might let something slip when in his cups. I wish he wouldn't drink so much.

I had my excuse ready. 'It's about the corpse in the boat, Uncle,' I said. 'It was a Maid of Honour who discovered it and she has it in her head it was a murder. Now the others are in such a twitter about being stabbed in their beds it has quite ruined my sleep, for they stayed awake all night in terror.' I had my fingers crossed behind my back at such a lie. I was glad he could not hear Lady Sarah snoring like a wild boar or Mary snuffling like a spaniel. 'I was hoping you might help me set their minds at rest, Uncle.'

Uncle Cavendish frowned with the effort of thinking so early in the day. 'Corpse?' he muttered. 'Boat?'

'Yes, Uncle,' I prompted him. 'You must remember! It was but yesterday. The body of the waterman, Will Stubbs, was brought in from the Frost Fair.'

He rubbed his beard. 'Ah, yes . . .' he said at last. 'The poor waterman. I'm afraid I cannot reassure your young ladies. The death was no accident. Will Stubbs was strangled – probably with his own neckcloth.'

I sucked in my breath. 'How do you know, Uncle?' I asked.

'There were marks of strangulation on the poor wretch's neck, and the cloth was pulled and strained. I am told it was the same cloth that was used to bind coins to his eyes.' Uncle Cavendish squeezed my shoulder. 'You are a sensible girl, Grace, and so I have told you the truth. But tell the other Maids it was an accident if it will give you back your sleep.'

'Thank you, Uncle,' I said. 'But what happens now? Will there be an inquest?'

'Yes, but it is a mere formality, Grace. There is no clue as to the murderer, so death by foul play will be pronounced and Will Stubbs's body returned to his family for burial.' Uncle Cavendish went over to a table and poured himself some wine.

It was time for me to take my leave.

I have come back to my chamber with a heavy heart. I am sorely disappointed that I've learned so little. I am no closer to discovering why Will Stubbs was murdered, or indeed, why two forged coins were bound to his eyes. I feel they must have been meant as a message to someone, for why blindfold a dead man in such a way? But a message to whom? And what can be the connection between poor Will Stubbs and the counterfeiters? These are the questions I must answer if I am to solve this mystery and find out who these counterfeiters are. I hope Ellie and Masou hear something today.

Hold fast! My uncle mentioned Will Stubbs's family. His widow may know more. Why did I not think of it before? I can go to see her and look for clues to the counterfeiting. I was the highest-ranking person (with their wits about them) at the scene when the body was discovered, so it would be quite natural for me to go and offer my condolences. Though Mrs Champernowne will have an apoplexy if I go alone.

Mary Shelton is stirring now. I will ask her to accompany me.

Past eleven of the clock, in the chapel

We have returned from our visit and scarcely in time for me to fetch my daybooke and penner and slip into the back of the chapel just as daily prayers began. I have kept my head bent devoutly. If I look up I'm bound to see someone glaring at me for being late! We are receiving a long, droning sermon from *The Book of Approved Sermons*. I can't imagine how anybody could approve of such lengthy texts! But at least I can write in peace for a while.

After breakfast, Mary and I got ready to skate along the river to Will Stubbs's cottage. It is on the north side of the Thames, at Myll Bank, just past the old Palace of Westminster. I asked Lady Ann Courtenay, one of Her Majesty's Ladies-in-Waiting, if she would arrange the necessary escorts for us, since it is quite improper for ladies to leave Court unattended. There is always a flock of gentlemen around, usually doing nothing and just waiting.

Lady Ann gave me a little hug and hurried off. Many of the Queen's Ladies knew my mother and have been very kind to me since her death.

Although I was most eager to discover more about the counterfeiting and the murder, I also wanted to bring some succour to the poor widow. So I decided to take a large basket of foods for the waterman's family.

When Mrs Barnes, the Pastry Cook, heard what I was about, she bustled around filling the basket. It made me feel quite hungry. There were raised pies, manchet bread, dried fruits and salt-fish fritters. I would love to have added an orange or two but unfortunately it is too early for oranges. Hopefully some will arrive from the lands of the Mediterranean in time for Christmas.

The basket looked most tempting when it was full, but then I remembered the poor fatherless children, so I added some of my ribbon sweets. I am very proud of myself for thinking of it.

Soon we were ready to set off with our escorts, Sir John Martin and Nicolas Bulmer. I wanted to giggle when they rushed over, very eager to please. They made a valiant attempt not to look too disappointed when they realized that Lady Sarah was not to be of the party.

We agreed to skate to Westminster because it would be much more fun than going by horseback down King Street. We were quite a merry group in spite of the biting cold and the sad event that had led to our trip. Sir John and Nicolas Bulmer were most entertaining and we passed a pleasant time on our journey.

Although I'm not sure the servant carrying the heavy basket agreed.

'I know you're up to something, Grace,' panted Mary as we went. 'You have that determined look in your eye. Are you doing something secret for the Queen?'

I was just wondering how to answer, for I did not really want to tell Mary the truth after Her Majesty had impressed upon me the need for secrecy, when Nicolas Bulmer slipped over and grazed his hand on the ice. Mary immediately rushed to bind up his wound with a kerchief, and I heaved a sigh of relief that I had not needed to reply. Mary is a good friend and keeps her counsel, but the fewer people who know what I am up to the better.

'Over there, my ladies,' said our servant suddenly, pointing at some mean cottages right on the riverside. 'That's where Will Stubbs lived, God rest his soul!'

The cottage was a low, dilapidated place with a rough thatch. I could see a sow snuffling about in a sty and chickens pecking round it. Our two escorts followed us up the path from the riverside.

'You have been most kind,' I said to them. 'Will you skate while we carry out our errand?' It would be much easier to talk to the family with just Mary and me and no awkward young gentlemen cluttering the place up.

Sir John and Nicolas Bulmer looked relieved and scuttled back to the ice as fast as they could.

The door was answered by a thin, pale woman, who we took to be Will Stubbs's widow, Margaret. She looked astonished to see two Maids of Honour at her house. I quickly introduced Mary and myself and explained the reason for our visit.

'Lord-a-mercy!' she gasped, bobbing a curtsy as she showed us into a small room that seemed to be full of children. 'Children, make way for these ladies – they come from the Queen herself, and look at the fine things they have brought us. Robert,' she called to a boy of about my age, 'get the jug of ale. Annie, bring those gingerbreads and almond tarts from the shelf. Jane, tell Uncle Harry about our guests.'

Mary Shelton and I sat down on a bench to sup our ale.

Mary started handing out the ribbon sweets to the children. Soon they were flocking round her and she was taken off to see the sow. Mary has many nieces and nephews and is always a favourite with children.

I glanced around. The cottage was very small and I could see almost all of it from where I sat. It was dark but clean, with fresh rushes on the floor, and the ale was of good quality. There was only one other room, and it looked as if the whole family slept in there. Rough straw palliasses and truckle beds covered the floor.

Just then, we were joined by another woman and a dour, heavy-set man. I looked at his face and nearly let out a cry of surprise. For a moment I thought it was Will Stubbs come back to life. The man took a glass of ale and stood in silence, staring hard at me.

'This is Harry, my husband's brother,' said Margaret.

That explained the likeness and, no doubt, why the man looked so mournful, I thought.

'And this is his wife, Susanna,' Margaret went on. 'Harry's a boatman, like my Will, and they live here with us. Harry works so hard – all hours, he does, and—'

'Now, Meg,' said Harry, putting a hand on her shoulder. 'Her Ladyship don't want to be hearing all about me.'

There was an awkward silence. I picked up a piece of embroidery that was lying on the table by my elbow. It was a gentleman's ruff. The linen was fine and the stitching exquisite. Little ox-eye daisies were worked into the material all round. 'This is lovely, Mrs Stubbs,' I said. 'Is it your own work?'

'Yes, my lady,' Margaret Stubbs replied eagerly. 'I work as a seamstress and lacemaker, and of course it is lucky I have my craft as I must provide for the children now that my poor Will has gone.' She dabbed at her eyes. 'It has so distressed us all – the manner of his death – when he was only trying to put an honest bit of food upon the table . . .'

'Come, come, don't upset yourself, Margaret,' said Susanna.

Her words were kind, but I wished she'd let her sister-in-law continue – I might have heard something useful. But I was already beginning to doubt that Margaret Stubbs knew anything of the counterfeit coins. She seemed a simple, honest woman, and she was clearly genuinely baffled by the manner of her husband's death. If the coins on Will's eyes had been meant as a message to someone, it obviously wasn't a message to his widow. And yet Will Stubbs must have some connection to the coins. Perhaps he was involved in the counterfeiting, but I couldn't suggest this to his poor grieving family. 'Who could have done such a thing to your husband?' I asked.

Before Margaret could answer Harry spoke up. 'We'll never know, my lady. We are Her Majesty's humble servants, as just wants to bury poor Will and let his spirit rest in peace.'

The children came bursting in at this point, with Mary Shelton in tow. They were chattering on about the sow and how she'd had ten piglets last spring and only trampled two, and how they hoped for more next year if a good boar could be found.

Although I had learned nothing of note, I saw that little would be gained by prolonging our visit. I managed to tear Mary away from her new friends and we took our leave.

When we had strapped our skates back on and joined the young men on the ice, we heard the three-quarter hour tolled from at least seven churches in turn, followed by the big bell in Westminster Abbey. We were going to be late for prayers if we weren't quick! I grabbed Mary's hand and pulled her across the ice. She shrieked as we went — I think it was with delight. She had never been so fast on skates.

By Heaven! Archbishop Parker himself is staring at me. I had better put down my penner. I do not wish to be accused of heresy!

Later this Day, some minutes after four of the clock

I am in my bedchamber. Mary Shelton and I are dressed in our best gowns. Tonight the Queen is entertaining the French Ambassador, Monsieur Bertrand de Salignac de La Mothe-Fénelon – what a mouthful! I hope there are not too many speeches. *Mon Dieu!* If he rambles on in French I shall nod off altogether.

Mary and I have been ready this last half of an hour. I am wearing the rose velvet gown which the Queen gave me for my thirteenth birthday and I'm feeling very grand. As usual, Lady Sarah is not dressed yet. She is sitting in her petticoat and arguing with Olwen, her tiring woman. She has bought a stinky new potion for her pimples from a stall at the Frost Fair, and Olwen is full of dire warnings about noses dropping off and skin turning green.

I am taking no part in all this. It gives me

time to write in my daybooke – and I have much to write.

When we came back from chapel I had very little heart for luncheon. All I could think of was how to learn more of Will Stubbs's death. Also, I had eaten plenty of sweetmeats at his family's cottage.

Since I had learned all I could from my visit there – and that was very little – I resolved to follow a different path. It is time to find out more about how coins are made, as that might give me clues as to how someone could make false money.

I decided to talk to Sir Edward Latimer. Who better than the Warden of the Queen's Mint to tell me what I needed to know? But I had to be careful not to tell him about the counterfeiting. It was going to be difficult to explain my sudden interest.

After luncheon the Queen bade us amuse ourselves as she had something dreary but important to discuss with Secretary Cecil. She didn't actually say that, but it was sure to be dreary.

We Maids of Honour sat by the fire in the Long Gallery. I thought it likely Sir Edward would come to Court this afternoon, to flirt with the Maids of Honour like the other young gentlemen, so I was keeping my eyes open for him.

'Let's sing some catches,' Penelope suggested. 'I'll start.' And she began with 'Hey-ho, Nobody at Home'. She has a pretty voice and we were all happy to join in when our parts came.

Then Lady Sarah stood up, looking rather pleased with herself. 'I have made up a new song,' she announced. 'I'll sing it and then you can all join in.'

When she was sure that everyone was look-ing at her, she began to sing to the tune of 'Of All the Birds That Ever I See'.

I thought it was a clever song so I've writ-ten it down. Then I won't forget it — although I'm sure Lady Jane would like to!

'Of all the maids that e-ver I see,
The Lady Jane Con-ings-by

Out up-on the ice did come,
But mostly ska-ted on her bum!'

Poor Lady Jane. Everybody burst out laughing. She had to smile and take it in good part in front of the young gentlemen, but I could see from her eyes that she was seething.

However, she soon had her revenge.

'I have a ditty,' she announced with a false smile. She sang it to the tune of 'Three Blind Mice' and looked hard at Lady Sarah as she did so, just in case we had any doubt as to the subject of the song!

'Three big spots, three big spots,
See how they grow, see how they grow,
They're spreading all over my lady's face,
She's running for potions all over the place,
Did ever you see such a—'

Mary Shelton, ever the peacemaker, quickly interrupted with a round of 'Hold Thy Peace', and we all joined in. Except for Lady Sarah and Lady Jane, who glared at each other. Then

Lady Sarah flounced off to find someone to flirt with instead. I think she had remembered that frowning made lines in her face.

Soon our mouths were parched from singing and we called for ale.

While we were drinking, Sir Edward appeared, sporting a fine brocade doublet with golden buttons. I seized the chance to talk with him.

I grabbed a beaker and offered it so quickly I nearly slopped ale down him. 'Sir Edward,' I gabbled, 'you look thirsty. We all know how hard you are working for Her Majesty at the mint.' I was most pleased with myself. I had got to the subject with my second sentence and no silly flirting or pretending to be a bear! I carried on. 'I would love to know how coins are made. Pray enlighten me.'

Sir Edward looked surprised for a moment. I suppose he had not expected a Maid of Honour to talk of anything so sensible. Then he gave me a courtly bow. 'I am greatly flattered that one of Her Majesty's own Maids of Honour should take an interest in my humble work,' he murmured to his knees. 'I feel like a common sparrow who has been favoured by a bird of paradise.'

I tried not to groan. All I wanted to do was find out how a coin was minted. Was I going to have to put up with all this flowery language and stare at the top of his head for ever? 'Arise, Sir Edward,' I said briskly. 'Now tell me, how do you get such beautiful designs onto the coins?'

'It is an involved matter, my lady,' he told me, 'and it would be most dull were I to describe it to you.'

He must have seen my face fall, for then he gave me a gallant smile. 'No, I have a much better idea,' he added. 'On the morrow I myself will take you to the Tower and you can enter the Royal Mint – where men transform silver into bright, sparkling likenesses of Her Glorious Majesty!'

Excellent! Surely I would find out something at the mint itself. 'I would like that very much, Sir Edward,' I replied.

'What would you like?' Lady Sarah interrupted.

Sir Edward swept her a bow and told her his plan.

'I would love to see the mint!' she gasped, with much fluttering of her eyelashes.

'So would I,' added Lady Jane, who had popped up behind her. 'But dear Lady Sarah, surely you have no gown fit to wear for such an occasion.'

'And you surely have no interest in the new coins of the realm, dear Lady Jane,' spat Lady Sarah. 'You have virtually told us so yourself!'

Sir Edward looked rather embarrassed – and quite comical – standing between the two furious Maids of Honour and not knowing what to do. Luckily Carmina, Penelope and Mary came over and demanded to join the party.

Sir Edward held up his hands in mock surrender. 'Ladies,' he gushed, 'it would give me the greatest of pleasure to escort you all to the Tower tomorrow and show you the splendours of the mint.'

And so now I cannot wait until tomorrow, even though I have to put up with the other

Maids of Honour hovering round Sir Edward.

Praise be! Lady Sarah is at last attired in her finery and we are ready to go down to the feast.

The Twenty-fifth Day of November, in the Year of Our Lord 1569

The Great Hall, eventide

It has been such a busy day and I have had no chance to write in my daybooke, so I have brought it to the Great Hall. We are having a special Frost Fair Masque. There is an intricate ice sculpture of a noble dragon – at least there was. It was put too near the fire. Now it looks like a deformed donkey!

Her Majesty is wearing a wonderful silver gown with pearls and diamonds sewn all over the skirt. The stomacher is embroidered with a design in blue and silver thread that looks like icicles. She has been crowned Monarch of the Ice and is in an excellent temper. Monsieur de La Mothe-Fénelon is paying her very pretty compliments and she is replying in her excellent French.

The black-and-white walls of the Great Hall

are draped in pure white silk and gauze, to make us feel as if we are inside an ice palace. And in the middle of the hall, Will Somers's troupe is entertaining us. Musicians are playing music with bells that sound like the tinkling of ice. French Louis, Gypsy Pete, and Peter and Paul, the dwarf twins, are leading the great company of tumblers. They are all dressed as snowflakes and icicles and are cartwheeling round the hall.

Masou looks splendid in his Jack Frost costume and mask, all silver sparkles. He is skidding and tumbling across the rushes on the floor, doing a wonderful likeness of a very bad skater on the ice. Everyone is laughing.

A few moments later ...

I had to lay down my daybooke just now. There was a great roll of drums and everyone fell silent. I couldn't help but watch what was going to happen.

'Beware!' cried Masou in ringing tones. 'The Spirit of the River is among us!'

Several of the ladies let out screams as a huge figure burst in through the doors. It was dressed in tarnished and muddied armour, with blue and green ribbons trailing like weed from its arms. It had a huge head and went among us, groaning and wailing.

Then the Queen stood up and strode to the centre of the hall. 'Desist, thou foul monster of the river!' she declaimed.

I love it when Her Majesty takes part in masques – and she nearly always does. She has a fine speaking voice which makes me go all tingly, and you are assured of a happy ending, for no one dare beat the Queen!

'O Monarch of the Ice, have pity on me,' growled the beast. He fell at her feet with a clatter that echoed round the hall.

Her Majesty placed her slippered foot upon his back. 'The Thames is conquered and held in thrall by my Reign of Frost!' she declared, and we all clapped and cheered and stamped our feet. She is truly magnificent.

Now I must try to concentrate or I will forget what I learned at the Tower today. I will write it all in order, and hope Masou does not try to put me off by pulling his usual faces at me as he capers by.

This forenoon Sir Edward arrived at Whitehall, looking very splendid on his gleaming black horse, and followed by his bodyguard and servants. Our mounts were brought to us in the court-yard. I was wrapped in my thick cloak and today made no quarrel with Mrs Champernowne about wearing my mask, for there was a bitter wind and the air is particularly biting when you're on top of a horse. Lady Sarah had found her mask, which was fortunate as she had a rather nasty rash on her cheeks and did not want Sir Edward to see it. I expect the rash came from the potion she bought at the Frost Fair. Olwen did warn her. I think Sarah was lucky she hadn't turned green and still had her nose.

'Follow me, ladies,' called Sir Edward, turning his horse towards the Court Gate with a flourish. 'I will take you on a journey of discovery.'

It is a long ride to the Tower – especially for those of us who don't like being on horse-back. We went up Lud Gate Hill, turned away from St Paul's towards the river and then along Thames Street.

As we rode out of Thames Street we finally came within sight of the Tower itself. We could see the long turreted ramparts of grey stone and the White Tower rising up beyond them. It was an impressive sight.

I noticed a small, straggly group of people clutching silver items and queuing outside the gate and along the side of the moat. I wondered briefly what they were doing there, but was too excited at the thought of what was within the walls to think about it for long. Soon I might find the clues I was searching for. I couldn't wait to see the mint.

We dismounted at the Bulwark Gate. Our grooms stayed with the horses, but Sir Edward's pages came with us. So did his bodyguard. Poor Sir Edward, thinking he needed protec-tion from Maids of Honour!

I expected us to go straight to the mint but

Sir Edward seemed to be keen to give us the Grand Tour of the Tower first. As soon as we had crossed the bridge over the moat and were inside the great walls he stopped. 'I have chambers here in the Byward Tower on the right,' he said, pointing to a twisting staircase that led up a small tower at the corner of the great castle walls. 'It is a fine dwelling with a view across the Thames. There is only one thing which mars my peace and it is that dratted bell.'

We looked up and saw a bell tower.

'When it tolls in the night it can make me jump from my bed,' Sir Edward told us.

Lady Jane tittered sympathetically and fluttered her eyelashes at him. But I thought it more likely that the noise from the two taverns near the base of the tower would interrupt his sleep.

Sir Edward led us through the arches of the Byward Tower towards yet another tower, this one named after St Thomas. Faith! The place should be named 'The Towers', for it is full of them! This one straddled the moat, and there was a tunnel that led out to the Thames, barred by an old, green-stained gate.

Sir Edward took us up some stairs into a large vaulted chamber and offered us mulled wine and sweetmeats to restore us after our long ride.

We took our masks off – except poor Lady Sarah of course. I nearly snorted my wine down my nose at the sight of her trying to drink without taking her mask far from her face.

Sir Edward made a pretty speech to welcome us to the Tower. I just wished he'd cut it short and take us straight to the mint, but there was no chance of that. So I gazed out of a window across the river. The Thames was not frozen here, to the east of London Bridge, and it was seething with barges, wherries, ferry boats and tall masted vessels.

At long last Sir Edward finished his speechifying. *Surely* we were going to the mint now!

'Ladies, shall I escort you to view the armouries?' he asked.

I stifled a groan. At this rate it would be midnight by the time we got there.

Then he saw our less than enthusiastic expressions. 'No,' he said quickly, ''tis, perchance, too frightening for such delicate guests.'

Offering Lady Sarah his arm, he led us back past the Byward Tower and along a cobbled way that was as busy as any street in London. Lady Jane walked stiffly behind them, with her nose in the air.

'This is Mint Street,' Sir Edward told us as he tripped along. 'The whole operation of the mint takes place within these buildings you see before you.'

The way was long, and followed the length of the outer wall, with single-storey buildings on either side. It was teeming with armourers, workmen, laundresses, maids and Yeomen Guard in their red uniform.

My stomach lurched with excitement. I knew I must keep my eyes open for anything suspicious. There might be someone working here who had a secret or two.

The first thing I noticed as we stepped through the low door into the silver melting room was how hot it was.

'Welcome to my domain, ladies,' said Sir Edward proudly, as his pages took our cloaks.

There was a huge roaring fire in the centre of the room and smoke rose up to a vent in the roof. A man in a leather tunic was putting silver plates, bowls and jugs into one of the melting pots that stood over the fire.

'Usually our silver comes from the Exchange and a little from our own mines in the West Country,' Sir Edward told us. 'However, the supply is not enough for our needs if we are to have Her Majesty's coin ready when she wills it. Therefore we are obliged to buy silver from the good folk of our fair City.'

So now I knew why there had been that queue of people outside the Tower. They'd been waiting to exchange their silver for some money from the mint.

Sir Edward took a battered old silver tankard and held it over one of the melting pots. 'I shall perform some magic for my esteemed guests,' he declared.

Ladies Sarah and Jane gasped prettily. They

looked as if they were hanging on Sir Edward's every word – but I wager they would have been hard pressed to remember any of it afterwards. Carmina and Penelope had begun chattering amongst themselves about the fine jewellery they would have with such a hoard of silver, and were paying no attention whatsoever.

'You will see,' continued Sir Edward, 'how a discarded drinking vessel such as this can become a brand-new coin of Her Gracious Majesty's realm.'

He passed the tankard to a labourer, who lowered it into the cauldron. Before our eyes the liquid silver swallowed it up.

'What happens now?' asked Mary Shelton.

'We make silver ingots,' explained Sir Edward.

Two workers took wooden poles and fitted them to the sides of one of the cauldrons. Then they carried the heavy pot in the fashion of a litter over to an iron tabletop on trestles. They rested the pot down and ladled the melted silver into long grooves in the iron. We watched the beautiful stream of liquid silver filling the grooves. Even Lady Jane looked fascinated at this.

'The ingots must be cooled, reheated and cooled again to strengthen the metal,' said Sir Edward. 'But that is a wearisome process to watch. Follow me and we shall see the silver beaten thin and cut into blanks.'

He led us into the next workshop, where five labourers were beating the silver ingots flat on anvils. The noise was deafening. Then we went through a third room, where men with shears were cutting the metal into small rough squares – which Sir Edward called 'blanks' – and throwing them into baskets.

'And finally, my ladies,' called Sir Edward, 'we shall see the magic completed. Please be so good as to go with me to the Press House.'

We followed a young boy, who staggered under the weight of a basket full of blanks. He took us outside and along to the last doorway in Mint Street.

'This is the gold and silver Press House,' announced Sir Edward. The room was large, with windows all down one side to let in as much light as possible. It was full of men toiling away at workbenches with large hammers.

The boy put down his heavy basket and ran between the benches, giving each man a handful of blanks.

Sir Edward went to the nearest workman. 'Dickon here will show you how we strike a coin.'

Dickon was not at all awed by the presence of noble young ladies. He grinned and showed us two long thick lengths of metal, each with a design on one end. 'These be called dies, your noble graciousnesses,' he told us. 'The end of each is pressed with the design for either side of the coin.' He held up one of the dies. 'This die we call the pile. Each pile is pressed with our blessed Majesty's likeness directly from Mr Anthony's engraving.'

I looked at the likeness. It was just as I remembered from the designs that Mr Anthony, the Mint Engraver, had brought to Her Majesty at Whitehall.

He rammed the spiked end of the pile into

his workbench and placed a blank on the top. Then he held up the other die. 'This be the trussel – see, it has the griffin pressed on its end.'

He placed the trussel so that the griffin design on the end of it was covering the blank. Holding it steady with his left hand, he took a hammer in his right and struck the top of the trussel, hard. Then he lifted the trussel away to reveal the griffin imprinted on the metal. He took a small pair of shears and trimmed the metal into a circle. Now it looked exactly like the coins the Queen had shown me.

'And there you 'ave it, my honourable-nesses!' he said, handing the coin around. 'With my skill I can do thirty of these a minute.' He stood up as if he were expecting applause like an actor at a play.

'Thank you, Dickon,' said Sir Edward quickly. 'That will do. Carry on with your work.'

I looked at the trimmings on the bench in front of me. 'What happens to all these spare pieces of silver?' I asked. I wondered if someone was managing to smuggle them out to be melted down for the counterfeit coins.

A pale man with a grey beard stepped forward. 'When the blanks have been cut, the trimmings are gathered, weighed and accounted for, my lady,' he said solemnly. He bowed. 'Jacob Petty at your service. I am Her Majesty's Master Moneyer. I oversee all the labourers.'

'All silver is carefully weighed by me first thing in the morning,' Sir Edward put in. 'And then the silver coins and trimmings are weighed again at the end of the day. The weight must always be the same. We cannot have any of it finding its way out of the Tower. And the trussels and piles are counted and locked safely away each night by good Jacob here, or myself. I am proud to say that nothing has gone missing while I have had the honour to hold this post.'

I was impressed. However flowery Sir Edward might appear, he was obviously a very conscientious Mint Warden. But I also felt quite baffled. How could anyone steal tools or silver in the face of such safeguards?

I glanced at Master Petty and caught him in the middle of a yawn. 'Forgive me, my lady,' he said quickly, covering his mouth. 'Work is hard here at present . . . but we are pleased to labour for Her Majesty,' he added hurriedly.

Mary Shelton was examining the Queen's face on the coin. 'Mr Anthony's engraving must have been very fine,' she said. 'For this is Her Majesty to the life!'

'I would have him engrave my likeness on a gold heart,' exclaimed Lady Jane, looking up coyly into Sir Edward's face. 'What think you, sir?'

I heard a grunt of annoyance from under Lady Sarah's mask.

Sir Edward gave a gallant bow. ''Tis a pity Derek Anthony is not here to receive your compliments,' he said to Lady Jane. 'I told him we had important visitors today, but he was suddenly called away to his workshop on urgent business, else he could have shown you the original engravings, which he keeps safe under lock and key here at the Tower.'

Everything seemed so safely locked up at

the Tower that I did not see how any counter-feiter could have smuggled anything out at all. I felt quite disconsolate on the way back to Whitehall. I am halfway through the time the Queen has given me, and yet no further forward in my investigation. Although at least I now know how coins are minted, and when I meet Sir Thomas Gresham again I can talk trussels and piles with some certainty!

Lord preserve us! I had quite forgotten that I am at a masque, but I have just been hit on the head by a walnut! I know who did that. Masou has a demonic grin on his face. He probably doesn't like it that I have had my head in my daybooke and have missed some of his antics. The Spirit of the River (Mr Will Somers, who has now removed his huge head-dress) is declaiming an ode about the Monarch of the Ice and her dominion over the Thames. The Queen is enjoying it hugely, for not only is it terribly flattering, but it is amusing also and Her Majesty loves to laugh. She is very fond of her fool, who can always be depended upon to entertain her. The old Will Somers, his father, served King Henry and she has made sure that the tradition is continued.

I must send Masou a sign. I would like to share all I have seen today with him and Ellie. And find out if they have managed to learn anything themselves . . .

I threw the walnut back at Masou as he capered past. I was very pleased with my shot as I caught him on the ear and he turned at once. 'Forgive me, Master Jack Frost,' I called. 'I was trying to juggle like you but I have not the skill.'

As I hoped, Masou came over. 'One walnut doth not a juggler make, my lady,' he said solemnly. Then he bent closer. 'What are you about, Grace?' he whispered, rubbing his ear. 'You've never bothered with juggling before.'

'Meet me tomorrow morning,' I whispered back. 'With Ellie. I'll be in the kitchen gardens when the clock strikes eight.'

Masou winked to show he had understood and cartwheeled away.

Now I will put my daybooke down and watch the rest of the entertainment.

The Twenty-sixth Day of November, in the Year of Our Lord 1569

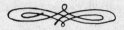

Morning – nine of the clock – in my chamber

I am to attend the Queen shortly. I hope I have time to finish this entry before I am called to the Presence Chamber. I am huddled by the fire in our bedchamber trying to warm up after my outing to the freezing kitchen gardens and back, along endless draughty corridors.

I dressed in my warm hunting kirtle, rushed through breakfast, hid some manchet bread in my sleeve for Ellie and crept down to the kitchen gardens as the clock in the courtyard was striking eight. As I passed the smokehouse, a hand shot out from the doorway and pulled me inside. Ellie put the sack back over the door and she and Masou and I made ourselves comfortable next to half a pig, which hung from the low ceiling.

'We can hide in here and be comfortable,' said Ellie. 'But we better be quick.'

It was warm inside the smokehouse and the smell of the smoked meat made me realize that my breakfast had been rather wanting. Then I remembered the manchet bread and passed it round.

Ellie seized her piece hungrily. 'What have you found out?' she asked, her cheeks bulging.

'But little,' I said miserably.

And Ellie and Masou had done no better. They'd heard nothing but unhelpful gossip, Ellie in the kitchens and Masou out at the Frost Fair where the body had been found.

As I hurriedly told them of my visits to the widow Stubbs and the Tower, we heard footsteps crunching on the frost outside. I'd hardly had time to get behind the pig before I heard the door open and Ellie demand, 'What d'you want in here, Joe?'

'I've come to check the hams,' came the reply. 'What are you two doing, more to the point?'

'None of your business, Joe Tucker,' laughed

Ellie. 'And if you tell anyone you found us here, I'll start spilling the beans about you and that new dairymaid.' I heard the footsteps hurry off.

'I thought that would make him blush,' said Ellie. 'You can come out now, Grace.'

'He will have it that you are my sweetheart now!' laughed Masou.

Ellie made a face. 'Well, at least he'll keep it to himself – and he didn't find Grace.'

Masou turned to me. 'Come, Grace, you say you have found out little but surely there is someone you suspect?'

'I feel it has to be somebody at the mint,' I told them. 'For that person would need to use the mint's own trussels and piles, or make their own from the original engravings, to produce such clever forgeries. But everything is kept so securely locked up.'

'Did you find out who has the keys?' asked Ellie, tearing off another piece of manchet bread.

'There aren't many,' I said. 'There's Jacob Petty – the Master Moneyer – who seems an honest and loyal worker. Although, strangely, he seemed very tired, as if he had been up all night. And then there is Sir Edward Latimer, the Mint Warden.'

'That maid in a man's garb!' snorted Masou. 'Surely he is too lily-livered. I have seen him about the Court. When anyone mentions the murder he nearly swoons with horror. And he can barely venture out without the protection of his bodyguard and pages.'

'That's as may be, but I reckon one of his pages is a thieving cur!' declared Ellie abruptly.

We looked at her in surprise.

'I nearly caught 'im in the act,' she continued dramatically. 'I was taking some collars to the starchers, when I sneaked a short cut through the Great Hall. One of Sir Edward's pages was in there, fingering a pretty silver chalice. I'm sure if I hadn't appeared he'd have had it away under his cloak!'

'You make a theatre of everything, Ellie,' laughed Masou. 'You should join our troupe. The poor lad had probably never seen anything so fine and was awestruck. Now, Grace, is there anyone else on your list of suspects?'

'Well, there is Derek Anthony, the Mint Engraver,' I said. 'He keeps the engravings safe. I know very little about him, for he was suddenly called away from the Tower before we arrived.'

'So how are any of these esteemed gentlemen linked to a humble waterman, the poor Will Stubbs?' asked Masou.

'Perchance Will Stubbs was just unlucky, and overheard something and then was killed so he couldn't tell,' I said. 'Though why the coins were put on his eyes—'

'Ellie!' We heard a coarse shout. 'Where is that lazy girl?'

'It's Mrs Fadget,' gasped Ellie, turning pale. 'She'll have my guts for garters if she thinks I've been shirking. I must go – and so must you.' And she fled from the smokehouse.

Fie! I have pressed so hard I have nearly torn the page, but I hate to see Ellie treated so. Mrs Fadget is in charge of the laundry at the moment as Mrs Twiste is unwell. She is always unkind to her, the old hag.

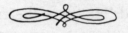

Later this Day

I am sitting on a hard bench at the tennis courts, where the young gentlemen of the Court are displaying their prowess to the French Ambassador – and to the ladies, *naturellement*. I'm supposed to be gasping at the antics of the players, who are whacking balls backwards and forwards – showing the French Ambassador how his native game should be played. To my mind it is like telling the Thames how to flow.

I have had a busy time since I made my last entry. To start with, I was nearly in great disfavour with Her Majesty, and it was all Mrs Champernowne's fault.

I was on my way to attend the Queen, after my meeting with Ellie and Masou, and I had plenty of time, when I bumped into the silly moo. She sniffed the air and then smelled my sleeve suspiciously. 'You stink like a smoked ham, Grace!' she snapped. 'What have you been up to?'

I had to think of an excuse. I'm sure Mrs Champernowne would go off like a firework if she found out that one of the Maids of Honour had been lurking in a smokehouse! 'I was walking the Queen's dogs,' I gabbled, 'and I must have gone too close to the kitchen bonfires. I'll go and change.'

'Look you do – and quickly!' she replied.

I rushed back up the stairs before she could think to ask me any more questions. I hadn't noticed the smell of the smoke lingering on me. I suppose my nose had got used to it.

Having changed into my second-best kirtle and gown, I was now in a terrible hurry. The Queen does not take kindly to tardiness, although she allows herself to be late when it suits. As I went past the door of the Presence Chamber, there was the usual mob of people waiting outside for an audience with Her Majesty. Secretary Cecil was among them, with his grave air and a bundle of papers. Several courtiers were waiting to beg favour. Then I recognized Derek Anthony, the Mint Engraver, at the back of the crowd. He was wearing a handsome ruff with little ox-eye daisies worked into the material all round. And I knew I'd seen that ruff before – in the widow Stubbs's cottage!

I felt as if someone had lit a candle in my brain. At last I had a link between one of my suspects and the murdered man! Of course, it might be mere chance that Her Majesty's Mint Engraver had bought a ruff from the widow of a man found dead with forged coins on his eyes, but it was also possible that it was some-thing more. I was most intrigued.

I considered what I knew of Derek Anthony. Sir Edward had told us that he was in charge of the original coin engravings, and that they were kept under lock and key at the Tower. But perhaps the engravings were *not* safely at the Tower. It could be that Derek Anthony was using them to set up another mint elsewhere. And mayhap Will Stubbs had found out about it. And then I remembered something else: when we were at the mint, Mr Anthony had been called away on 'urgent business' – or so he'd told Sir Edward. Perchance that was because he knew we would want to be shown the engravings and they were not at the Tower!

I caught up with Her Majesty in the Privy Gallery, where she was showing the French Ambassador some of the treasures of Whitehall Palace. The Maids of Honour were following dutifully and looking bored. I had meant to slip in among them quietly, in the hope that the Queen would not know I'd been missing, but I was thinking so hard about Derek Anthony that I came face to face with Her Majesty, the Ambassador and a bust of Attila the Hun, before I knew what I was about.

Her Majesty pursed her lips and glared at me because I was late – her expression made Attila look like a friendly lapdog.

I curtsied and backed away quickly to join the other Maids. They all gave me strange glances and Lady Jane pointedly held her nose.

'Fie, Grace!' whispered Mary Shelton. 'Have you been buying noxious potions like Lady Sarah? You smell of wood ash.'

Hell's teeth! I realized I must have got smoke in my hair as well as in my clothes. But I was too preoccupied to worry about that. My mind was racing. The Queen would be hours impressing the Ambassador – Whitehall Palace is full of treasures and each one has a history. On any other day my heart would have sunk at the prospect of trailing round after Her Majesty as she told each tale with relish, but today I was heartily glad that she had so many paintings and statues and vases, for it meant that Derek Anthony would be at Court most of the day, waiting to see the Queen. And this had given me an idea.

While he was away from his workshop I could go there and have a look around for clues. But first I needed to get permission from the Queen to leave Court.

I had my chance when Monsieur de La Mothe-Fénelon stopped to admire the painting of a goldsmith's wife.

'*Mon Dieu, qu'elle est belle!*' he murmured, forgetting the Queen for a minute.

It wasn't surprising. It is said that the woman

in the picture was a mistress of the Queen's father, and every gentleman who saw the painting would stop and exclaim at how beautiful she was.

I knew I had a few moments before he recovered his wits. 'Your Majesty,' I said quickly, 'will you grant me permission to leave Court? I am in urgent need of a seal bearing my coat of arms.'

The royal eyebrows rose. No one ever dared leave a Royal Tour!

'I have very good reason,' I added, looking meaningfully at her and hoping she would take the hint. 'Your Mint Engraver has done such fine work on your coin that I would visit his workshop.'

Thank goodness the Queen is quick-witted. The eyebrows went down and she gave me a slight nod. She had obviously understood my real meaning. 'Are you certain that it is he you should be seeking?' she asked.

I was having a coded conversation with the greatest ruler on earth and no one else knew what we were really talking about! 'I am not certain, Your Majesty,' I answered carefully. 'But I have heard much of his workshop and wish to see it as soon as possible, even though Mr Anthony himself awaits an audience with you here in the palace.'

'I fear Mr Anthony may have to wait here many hours until I am at liberty to see him,' said Her Majesty with a knowing look. 'However, I grant you leave, Grace, but go not unattended.'

I think she was about to insist I took a great retinue with me, when the French Ambassador remembered his manners and turned to her.

'*Naturellement*, Her Glorious Majesty outshines even the most beauteous of ladies,' he gushed.

The Queen turned at this flattery, and with deep curtsies I made my escape and headed for the laundry. I had my own ideas about who should be my retinue.

When I got to the washroom I went straight over to the Deputy Laundress. 'Mrs Fadget,' I said in my most imperious voice, 'I have need of Ellie. She must come with me in all haste to wash a precious silk handkerchief of the Queen's which Her Majesty will not allow to be taken from her chamber.'

Ellie, who had been scrubbing away at a washboard, dried her hands and hurried over eagerly.

'You don't want that idle little baggage, my lady,' said Mrs Fadget, beginning to take off her apron.

I saw Ellie's face fall.

'Her Majesty will be wanting someone of experience with fine cloth,' Mrs Fadget went on. 'I shall come with you.'

'The Queen was most insistent it should be Ellie,' I told her.

Mrs Fadget looked astounded at this.

'Ellie has small gentle hands just right for the task,' I explained hurriedly.

Mrs Fadget looked down at her huge, sausage-shaped fingers, gave a grudging curtsy and bustled off crossly.

'Did Her Majesty really say that about me?' gasped Ellie as we left the laundry and made our way to my bedchamber.

'No, I'm afraid she didn't, Ellie,' I said. 'It was the only way I could think of to get you away from there.'

Ellie looked disappointed.

'But I'm sure she will one day, when you are Chief Laundress,' I added. 'I don't feel guilty about telling a lie to that nasty old harpy, because I need you and your sharp eyes – and it truly is on the Queen's business.'

Ellie's eyes widened when I told her we were going to Derek Anthony's workshop. 'Mr Anthony has an apprentice,' she told me. 'Matthew by name. All us servants know him. He's got quite a reputation amongst the girls.' She blushed. 'Indeed, he carries a torch for me!'

I nudged her. 'Lucky you, Ellie – an engraver for an admirer. Perhaps he'll do you a likeness.'

'Get away!' exclaimed Ellie. 'He may carry a torch for me, but I don't care a fig for him.'

'Now,' I said, 'it must seem that I am visiting the workshop to ask about a seal for my coat of arms. It will give us a chance to snoop around and look for anything suspicious. You will pretend to be my attendant – I'll lend you a gown.'

'One of your gowns!' gasped Ellie. 'I'll be quite the fine lady.'

When we reached my bedchamber, I laid out my gowns – apart from the rose velvet one – for Ellie to choose from. It was fortunate that she was not choosing one of Lady Sarah's for we would have been all day about it.

Ellie sighed as she fingered the fine fabrics. 'I've always favoured this green one. It is so lovely . . .'

I was helping her to put it on when there was a knock at the door. Ellie jumped in surprise and ran to hide behind my bed curtains, while I went to the door.

Olwen had brought me a message from Mrs Champernowne. 'You're to go to the Holbein Gate when you're ready, my lady,' she told me. 'Mrs Champernowne has arranged an escort for you.'

My heart sank. I had hoped that Ellie and I would be able to carry out my mission without the company of any silly young gentlemen. But, alas, it was not to be.

Olwen tidied away some of Lady Sarah's kirtles, picked up a sleeve that needed stitching and then hurried away down the corridor.

Ellie emerged from her hiding place and I quickly finished helping her to dress. Once she was laced into the gown, we took one look in Lady Sarah's looking glass and burst out laughing. Although she is my age, Ellie is shorter and thinner than me, and the dress fairly swamped her.

'Don't worry, Ellie,' I said. 'We'll try a bum roll under it and we'll pin the rest up.'

Even so, the finished effect was rather bunchy and the skirt threatened to trip her up when she walked. But it made my heart glad to see her sweeping around the room like a lady, and we were able to make do with a cloak over the top. I lent her my velvet mask and borrowed Mary Shelton's for myself.

I made Ellie wear the mask until we left the palace, as there would be terrible trouble if anyone found out what she was doing.

We made our way down to the Holbein Gate and King Street, where we came upon Mrs Champernowne with two young gentlemen courtiers holding the bridles of their horses, and a litter with four littermen.

'Blimey, Grace,' whispered Ellie. 'Are we going in that? I'll feel like a proper princess.'

For one horrible moment I thought Mrs Champernowne was coming with us too. She stared long and hard at Ellie and I thought she had recognized her. Then she shrugged. 'The Queen said you were running an errand for her, Grace,' she said sternly. 'And she insisted that Sir Simon and Mr Robin Middleton accompany you. I don't know why – Lord knows, they're not the brightest stars in the firmament. Just make sure you behave, look you.'

Once Mrs Champernowne had finished telling me what I should and shouldn't do, and bustled off to fuss over the other Maids, I introduced Ellie to the gentlemen as my attendant. Soon she and I were being carried along King Street in the litter towards the Charing Cross.

Sir Simon and Robin, his younger brother, rode along beside us. They seemed rather tongue-tied in our presence.

'I wish we could go alone,' I muttered to Ellie. 'How can we look for clues with these two in attendance?'

'Don't worry about that, Grace,' Ellie whispered back. 'There's a very welcoming tavern called the Ship Inn close by. I'm sure we could nudge them into spending an hour or so there.'

'That's a good idea, Ellie – but you'd better let me do the talking in front of the gentlemen of the Court,' I told her firmly.

'Don't you think I talk proper then?' demanded Ellie, with a twinkle in her eye.

Ellie was enchanted by the journey. She sat in front, holding the curtains wide open, and kept turning round and pointing out the wonders of London.

'But you've seen all this many times!' I reminded her.

'Not like this I ain't!' she sighed. 'I'm always on foot, and busy watching out for the dung and the rubbish.'

At last we arrived at West Cheap and the littermen stopped. Our companions helped us out with much blushing.

West Cheap was as busy and bustling as ever, full of customers going in and out of the apothecaries and grocers' shops. A young servant passed us carrying a basket, and we smelled the sweet scent of the dried lavender she had just bought.

I had forgotten just how many goldsmiths and engravers there are in this street. I had to look hard among the signs to find the one that said DEREK ANTHONY. His workshop was at the bottom of a tall, five-storey building, and it had a heavy studded door and a large front window.

As Ellie had said, the Ship Inn was just over on the other side of the street. The smell of roasting meat hung pleasantly on the cold air and Ellie licked her lips. I hung onto her arm to try and bring her back to the matter in hand, and beckoned to one of our companions. 'Sir Simon,' I said, peeping coyly round my mask. 'It will be tedious for you to stand by as I deliberate over the design for my seal.' I hoped I sounded a little like Lady Sarah, for I wanted to persuade him to do as I wished. 'Why don't you and your gallant brother step up to the inn and bespeak a noontide meal for us all. We shall be but an hour at most.'

The two young men looked pleased at this suggestion and dashed over to the inn like two cantering ponies.

Ellie and I pushed open the heavy door and stepped into Mr Anthony's establishment. The shop was large, with an opening at the back showing a workshop beyond. On the walls were charts displaying engraving designs for customers to choose from. Near the window was an empty ware bench with a cabinet behind it, and at the side stood a counting table.

'Don't think much of this,' muttered Ellie from under her mask. 'There's nothing for sale!'

'An engraver cannot leave his wares out,' I told her. 'They are far too valuable.'

At the sound of our voices a young man came out from the workshop, wiping crumbs from his mouth. He was wearing a thick leather apron, and had a thatch of brown hair and piercing blue eyes. 'What an honour, your ladyships,' he said with a deep bow. 'I'm Matthew Tibbit, apprentice to Mr Anthony, and in charge while he has stepped up to the palace on business.' Then he gave a start of surprise as Ellie removed her mask. 'Ellie Bunting!' he exclaimed. 'What are you doing 'ere, dressed so fine? And who's this?' he added, pointing his thumb at me and grinning. 'The palace dairymaid?'

I swept my mask aside. 'I am Lady Grace Cavendish, one of the Maids of Honour to Her Majesty the Queen,' I said sternly. 'I am here to commission a new seal bearing my coat of arms.'

Matthew instantly looked horrified. 'I–I beg your pardon, my lady,' he stammered. 'I am ever at your service. I'm as good an engraver as any you'll find in London – and better than most.'

I could see that Ellie was trying not to laugh and it nearly started me off. 'I was hoping to see Mr Anthony,' I said, 'for I was very impressed with the fine designs he produced for the Queen's new coin.'

'Faith, your ladyship,' laughed Matthew, 'it was me who did most of the work on that! Indeed, if it wasn't for me this place would grind to a halt! I'm the first one 'ere of a morning and the last one to leave at night. Honest worker, that's me.'

'In that case,' I said, 'you can be the one to help me. I was thinking of a seal on a gold ring.'

'You're talking to the right man then, my lady,' said Matthew, cheerfully leading us to the ware bench. 'I do all the rings.' He carefully laid a velvet cloth on the bench. Then he unlocked the cabinet with a key from his belt and took out a seal ring. 'This'll impress you, Ell,' he said, giving her a nudge. 'And you, your ladyship,' he added hurriedly.

I pretended to examine the ring closely as Matthew chattered on.

'It's this year's fashion,' he said importantly. 'Most recently favoured by Lord Howard of Effingham himself. I did all them laurels.' He looked about furtively. 'I do extra work – not quite as expensive as Mr Anthony, if you get my meaning. I could do you a seal that would be the envy of the Court for half the price he'd charge.'

So Matthew was not the honest worker he claimed to be. This was getting more interesting by the minute. But I needed to be free of him so I could have a good snoop round. 'Thank you, Master Tibbit,' I said, waving him away. 'I would like a little time to consider.'

'Of course, my lady,' answered Matthew, turning back to the cabinet. 'Now, there is also this ring, modelled in the French style . . .'

As he picked up the ring, I made a desperate face at Ellie, hoping she would understand that I needed her to distract Matthew. Thankfully she caught my meaning straight away.

'Oh, Matthew,' she cooed, 'you're so clever. Show me some more of your work.'

Matthew couldn't resist. He immediately took Ellie's arm and guided her to the other end of the ware bench. 'I've got some earrings 'ere that I'm making for a foreign princess,' he boasted.

I took my chance and walked around the shop, pretending to look at the designs on the wall. Then I sidled over to the door that led to the workshop.

In a flash, Matthew popped up again like a jack-in-the-box. 'Now, if you would come back to the ware bench, my lady, I can show you—'

'Matthew!' called Ellie, holding up an earring and placing it by her ear. 'What do you think? Queen of the May?' She smiled at him in the way I'd seen Lady Sarah and Lady Jane smile at the young men of the Court.

Master Tibbit was obviously torn between flirting with Ellie and serving a noble client.

I nodded at him. 'I would be glad if you would do me the honour of attending to Ellie,' I said solemnly.

Matthew shot back to her side and I seized the opportunity to slip through the doorway into the workshop. I could hear Ellie giggling and doing a fine job of keeping Master Tibbit's attention from me.

There were two workbenches strewn with tools, and in the corner stood a large chest. On one of the benches burned a candle and I could see that the tools had been swept aside into a rough pile, with pieces of gold and silver filigree among them. In the middle, in pride of place, was a trencher with the remains of an eel pie on it, and a half-full tankard of ale. Matthew was obviously taking advantage of Mr Anthony's absence to do very little work. I quickly sorted through the tools on both benches, but I could find no trussels or piles such as we'd been shown at the Tower, only fine etching tools and tiny shears.

I crept to the door and listened carefully. My next move would be a bold one and I did not want to be disturbed.

'You do know how to flatter a girl,' I heard Ellie giggle. 'You're making me blush!'

'And I'll make those pretty cheeks pink again if you'll come to the White Boar Inn tonight. I've got a bit of business to do first, but then I'll be all yours,' I heard Matthew saying.

I tiptoed over to the chest and eased the lid open. Then I took the candle to help me make out what was inside. Piled up at one end were wax tablets with designs on them – but none were of coins. Next to them was a stack of accounting books and some engraved table knives lying on a wooden board – and there was something underneath the board.

Trying not to make any noise, I gently lifted it out to see what was beneath. I saw a shape wrapped in linen – it looked big enough to be hiding the counterfeiters' dies! My hand trembled with excitement as I carefully unwrapped the material. I held the candle close. There inside lay two large, greasy sausages! It seemed that Master Tibbit had saved some of his lunch for later.

I put the sausages back and sighed. I could find nothing to link Mr Anthony with coin forgery.

I returned to the shop in time to hear Matthew declare, 'I've always got a purse full of money, Ellie. You'd do well to stick with me.' He was leaning close to Ellie and had his arm round her shoulders.

'Master Tibbit,' I said, making the cheeky lad jump, 'I fear I need more time to consider, and must return to the palace forthwith. Come, Ellie.'

Ellie looked very relieved and immediately scampered to my side.

'Now, my lady,' said Matthew coaxingly, 'what is there to consider? You won't find finer work than mine. And don't forget I offer special terms' – he gave a sly nod – 'which we don't mention to Mr Anthony.'

'I will not forget it,' I said gravely. We put on our masks and swept out.

'And remember I'll be in the White Boar tonight, Ellie,' I heard Matthew call after us as we crossed to the Ship Inn.

A few minutes later we were facing each other over a table heaving with veal pies, roasted capons, pasties and mead. The young gentlemen had done us proud and Ellie's eyes looked as if they were about to pop! Luckily for us, the gentlemen had heard of a cockfight in the next street and begged permission to go and watch for a few minutes. I told them they were very welcome to watch such sport, so long as we didn't have to hear about it afterwards.

'Well, Ellie,' I said, 'your young admirer seems to be a man of wealth.'

Ellie finished a mouthful of pie and wiped her mouth on her sleeve. 'He's not my admirer,' she said. 'Well, maybe he is a bit. Pass me some of that bird. Anyway, did you find anything in the workshop?'

'Not a thing.' I sighed. 'I can find no evidence to show that Mr Anthony is the counterfeiter. However, Matthew is a different matter.'

'Why's that?' asked Ellie.

'He's not an honest worker,' I replied. 'He does work without his master's knowledge and he has a purse full of money. He could have made his own dies from Mr Anthony's coin engravings – before his master took them to the Tower – and been paid handsomely by the counterfeiter.'

'Just my luck,' laughed Ellie, 'to have a villain for an admirer! How are you going to find out for sure?'

'You and I are going to spy on him tonight!' I declared. 'We'll follow him to the White Boar and find out about this "bit of business" he was so eager to mention.'

Ellie nearly choked on a piece of capon. 'What?' she spluttered. 'I've never had such a day in my life!' She took a swig of mead and fanned herself with her mask. 'Cor, to think of it: Lady Grace and Lady Ellie doing a bit of snooping in the dark.'

'We have to go unaccompanied, so we can't be ladies!' I said. 'We'll have to think of a disguise.'

Ellie's face fell. I think she wanted to keep the fine gown on for as long as she could. 'I've grown out of that gown,' I insisted, 'so you can keep it.'

For a moment Ellie's eyes shone, then she shook her head. 'I can't, Grace,' she said sadly. 'Folk will think I've thieved it. I'll get in terrible trouble and be thrashed, for sure.'

Just then, the young gentlemen returned to accompany us back to the palace, but they were too busy boasting of their winnings at the cockfight to pay us much attention.

I noticed Ellie was walking very stiffly back to the litter, holding her skirts awkwardly. 'What's wrong?' I asked, when we were behind the curtains. 'Are you in pain?'

'I will be later,' she grinned, lifting up her gown to reveal three pasties and half a pie! 'I'm going to have a right royal belly ache!'

So tonight, after supper, I am going to slip out with Ellie to follow Matthew Tibbit. This time, both Ellie and I will be disguised as boys and I am very excited. I'm a bit scared too. If Matthew turns out to be involved with counterfeiters then he is likely also involved in murder!

And now the gentlemen have tired of tennis, and Mary Shelton is suggesting that we return to our chamber, so I must stop.

Later this Day – eleven of the clock – in my chamber

Lady Sarah is talking in her sleep – or should I say *flirting* in her sleep? I keep hearing her say, 'Fiddlesticks, Sir Robert!' and 'How witty, Lord Crispin!' Lady Jane would be jealous. Even in her dreams Lady Sarah is surrounded by young gentlemen!

I am huddled next to the fire. I have promised Olwen that I will dampen it down when I retire. I must not forget. I am so tired that I want to go straight to my bed but I must write down this night's events.

After supper this evening, the other Maids settled to play cards and I crept down to join Ellie in the starch room. This is where Ellie sleeps most nights and it is not a comfortable chamber. Mrs Fadget spends much of the day in here, as she is the starch mistress, but thankfully there was no sign of her now.

It would not be safe for two young female servants to be out together at night, so Ellie and I got dressed up as boys. She'd 'borrowed' a jerkin, hose and breeches from the spit boy in the kitchen for me. She wouldn't tell me where she'd found the jacket she brought me, and I didn't want to ask. The clothes were a tight fit, rather smelly and very itchy, even though I wore two shirts underneath!

Masou had plunged my riding boots into a compost heap to make them look old and tatty — and to make me smell even more, I think! My hair is still short after my last escapade as a boy on Her Majesty's business, so it looked quite appropriate under the cap that Ellie found for me. Ellie said it made me look quite the ragamuffin and I think even the Queen would not have recognized her Lady Pursuivant.

Then Ellie produced another pile of clothes and pulled them on. I held my nose. These were even smellier than mine.

'I got them from the stable lad,' she told me. 'Not that he knows, of course!'

We went out into the freezing night air and hurried past the guards at the Holbein Gate. It is amazing how invisible servants are, for no one challenged us.

To begin with, I enjoyed the freedom of walking in boys' clothes. But I was tired by the time we had gone all the way through Covent Garden fields to the City and had reached Milk Street, where the White Boar Inn was. And the thin clothes of a spit boy were no good for keeping the bitter cold out. I began to despair of ever feeling my hands again.

We pushed through the crowds at the door to the White Boar and crept in, finding ourselves a quiet corner from which to look around and observe. There was no sign of Matthew.

'Have we missed him?' whispered Ellie.

'I hope not,' I whispered back.

At that moment the door of the tavern burst open and Matthew swaggered in.

'Make way for the next Royal Engraver!' he exclaimed. Several girls ran over to him and he was soon seated at a table with a brimming tankard of ale in his hand.

'You're lucky to have my company, ladies,' he boasted in a loud voice. 'Now, buy us another drink, and maybe I'll bring along a fine gold necklace tomorrow night, for the one who treats me best.'

'Don't you believe him, girls,' muttered Ellie, as we crept nearer and hid behind a partition next to his table.

Matthew seemed to be drinking a great deal, but I noticed he did not put his hand in his purse once. He paid court to every girl in the tavern by promising them riches and doffing his cap – which was very fine and adorned with a beautiful peacock's feather.

After a while he took his leave and began to barge his way out.

'I didn't see him do any business there,' Ellie hissed. 'Did we miss it?'

'No,' I said. 'He must mean to do it else-where. Let's follow.'

We pushed through the busy throng, trying to keep him in our sights while darting along the shadowy streets and dodging the dung that covered the cobbles. I had never realized quite how disgusting and smelly these small City streets are. First a drunken old man barged into us. Then someone opened a casement and threw out a bucketful of dirty water, which sent a couple of scavenging cats racing for cover and only just missed us! I am glad to be a Maid of Honour and travel everywhere by litter, or on horseback!

It was the same story in the next inn, and the next. Matthew boasted loudly as he drank more. He was able to find a pretty girl to buy him a drink at every tavern.

'I don't think Matthew is constant to you, Ellie,' I grinned, as we pressed our noses up against the glass and peered into the Old King Lud. This tavern was heaving with people and we couldn't get inside.

'You're right, Grace,' said Ellie grumpily, watching Matthew put an arm round yet another girl. 'He don't seem to be missing me! I reckon he was lying about having lots of money as well. He hasn't paid for a single drink— Look out, he's coming.'

Matthew staggered out and wobbled down a dark alley to yet another inn. When he reached the door, he lurched in and seemed to be making for some pretty girls in the corner. But his drunken legs wouldn't carry him any further and he slumped down at the nearest table.

We slipped in, and found seats by the wall close to Matthew, where there was no candle-light to betray us. I was feeling very tired and my eyes started to close.

Suddenly, Ellie nudged me awake. 'Who's that?' she whispered.

A man wrapped closely in a black cloak pushed his way through the crowd and sat down at Matthew's table. I grabbed Ellie's arm in excitement. 'This must be the bit of business he boasted of,' I whispered back. 'Listen hard! It could be about the counter-feiting.'

'I've been searching for you all over the City!' growled the man. 'You said you'd meet me tonight.'

'Well, I've been busy,' protested Matthew.

'I'm going to be the best engraver in the world, y'know—'

'Don't give me all your fancy talk, Matthew Tibbit,' snapped the man in the cloak. 'I knows you too well. You're just an apprentice — and not a very good one at that. Have you brought me what we agreed?'

Matthew began fumbling for his purse.

'Do you think he's getting counterfeit coins out?' Ellie whispered in my ear.

Matthew looked round to make sure no one was listening. 'I've had a bit of trouble,' he muttered.

'Trouble?' The stranger did not sound pleased.

'I haven't got all the money yet.' Matthew slapped some coins on the table. 'You'll have to make do with these for now.'

I leaned forwards, trying to see what he had put down, but I couldn't. My heart was thudding like horses' hooves. Were we going to learn something of the counterfeiters at last?

The man took one look and stood up angrily, knocking his chair flying. 'I'm never doing business with you again, Matthew Tibbit!' he shouted. 'When I made you that fine cap, you swore to pay me the whole fifteen shillings by last Friday se'nnight. And all you can give me is two measly groats and a penny!' He pushed the table aside roughly, snatched the cap from Matthew's head and barged his way out through the crowd.

Ellie and I looked at each other.

'I don't think Matthew Tibbit has anything to do with the counterfeiting,' I said sadly. 'He just likes to give the impression that he's involved in grand schemes. But he isn't clever or cunning enough to manage a counterfeiting scheme as grand as the one we've discovered.'

'He's nothing but a braggart,' agreed Ellie. 'There's naught in his head but air.'

'We've had a wasted evening,' I sighed wearily. 'Let's go back to Whitehall.'

'Look on the bright side, Grace,' said Ellie as we left the inn. 'At least he's one less suspect to worry about.'

And now here I am back in my chamber,

and scarcely further forward with my investigation. And I have but one more day! I hate to think that I may fail the Queen when she has put so much faith in me and defended me to Sir Thomas Gresham. And it makes my blood boil that someone is seeking to defraud Her Majesty and our country. I think it is downright treachery!

Ellie and I have arranged to meet Masou in the morning to think about what to do next. But at the moment I am mystified. Perhaps a good night's sleep will help. I am tired enough to sleep for a fortnight. I pray we find out something tomorrow.

The Twenty-seventh Day of November, in the Year of Our Lord 1569

Late forenoon

I am writing this while sitting upon my bed, trying not to fall asleep. I am so tired this morning. Last night I had just got into bed and begun to feel warm when I remembered I had forgotten to dampen the fire. I had to leave the comfort of my bed to do it, which woke me right up, and I swear I heard the clock strike three before I finally fell asleep. And now I have this one day to solve the mystery and I fear I will never do it!

After breakfast I put on my black kirtle and cloak and collected the Queen's dogs – for it is one of my duties (and pleasures) to walk them.

They looked surprised and not too pleased that I would take them out on such a bitter morning, but I needed the excuse. And when they found that they were not just going to chase round the lavender hedges in the Privy Garden, they soon forgot the cold and began to bark excitedly, straining at the leash as we went down the passageways to the Tilting Yard. They could smell their favourite walk beyond – the park at St James's. I threw frosty sticks for them until Henri, the Queen's favourite, found a rabbit hole. That kept him and Philip and Ivan (who really is rather terrible, like the Tsar of all the Russias) busy for an age. I love Her Majesty's dogs and they always cheer my spirits no matter how doleful I feel.

Masou and Ellie were under some trees. I wondered what excuse Ellie had used to leave the laundry room. She was shivering with the cold. Masou was peeling the bark back from some sticks so that they looked like miniature fountains.

'What are you up to?' I asked.

'You'll see,' said Masou. He laid the sticks in a pile and got out his tinder box and flint.

I laughed. 'You'll never make a fire like that. The wood's far too damp.'

'Oh, won't I, Miss Wiseacre?' he said, with a wink at Ellie. A thin spiral of smoke was rising from the sticks and in no time at all they were aflame.

Ellie clapped her hands and huddled up to it.

'Is it some sort of African magic?' I asked.

'Nothing so mysterious,' said Masou. 'It is only the bark that is damp. Inside, the wood is quite dry.'

'Fie on you, Masou!' exclaimed Ellie. 'You make it sound like you thought of it yourself, when it was little Gypsy Pete that taught you to do it!' She gave Masou a push.

Grinning, Masou pretended to overbalance, did a backflip, landed nimbly on his feet and stuck his tongue out at us.

'Well, perhaps Master Clever Clogs can ask Gypsy Pete to solve this problem,' I said, as we squatted by the fire. 'I have but today to catch the counterfeiters and no clues! We found nothing at the Tower, or at Derek Anthony's workshop, or from Matthew Tibbit, or from Will Stubbs's cottage. I thought, when I saw

Mr Anthony wearing the ruff made by Mrs Stubbs, that we would soon have this matter solved.' I sighed, remembering the bereaved family. 'At least Mrs Stubbs can keep her children by her sewing. She was so kind, when we visited. There she was, newly widowed, and yet she took the trouble to make us welcome and offer us fine ale and sweetmeats.'

Ellie's mouth dropped open. 'Fine ale and sweetmeats?' she queried. 'You never said that before. Watermen's families don't have enough money for fine ale and sweetmeats. Especially now the river is frozen and they can't ply their trade. And the earnings of a seamstress are paltry. They must have money coming from somewhere else. Perchance it is from the counterfeiting!'

I felt mortified. 'I am too used to living at Court to pick up on such clues,' I said sheepishly. 'Well done, Ellie! We are getting somewhere at last!'

'Mayhap those who live close by might know something,' said Ellie, huddling close to the fire.

'Then I must go back there and speak with them,' I declared.

'Common folk won't talk to a fine Maid of Honour,' said Masou. 'It's not their place, and you will find them close-mouthed in their shyness.' He pulled two flaming sticks from the fire and began to juggle with them. 'If you go you must be in disguise and I will come with you.'

'Not the spit boy's clothes again,' I moaned. 'I'm still itching and I got so cold.'

'Spit boy!' Masou's eyes gleamed with mock horror. 'Nothing so lowly, my lady! I have a much better notion. We shall dress as pedlars and sell our wares upon the ice, near the cottage. People will tell pedlars all their secrets – for they are here today and gone tomorrow.'

I wasn't sure that the duds of a pedlar would itch much less than a spit boy's, but I had to own it was a very good plan. 'What excuse will you use to come with us, Ellie?' I asked.

'I can't get away again,' sighed Ellie. 'Mrs Fadget looked mightily peeved when I pretended you'd called for me to go to your bedchamber this morning so I could come out here. I think she hasn't forgiven me for being chosen over her to deal with the Queen's handkerchief.'

Poor Ellie. I could imagine Mrs Fadget would deal out some unkindness – and all for a handkerchief that had never been.

Masou kicked the fire out and I whistled for the dogs.

It took me some while to persuade Henri and his band of canine rogues that Mr Rabbit was not at home. I fair had to drag them back on their leashes. It was amusing to see their paws scrabbling on the slippery ground, but they were no match for me (in the end!).

So here I am in my bedchamber, waiting for Masou and Ellie to sneak up with my disguise. I am planning to pretend to come down with a chill and take to my bed very shortly. I have stuffed my spare kirtles under my bedcovers and I am pleased that – if someone were to look behind the curtains – it does look as if someone is asleep in there.

I may yet solve this mystery.

We are back from our peddling and I must write all that occurred this afternoon before I have to get ready for supper, for we have made great progress with our investigation. I fear my writing may be something of a scrawl as all my thoughts want to tumble out at once. Mary Shelton has gone to tell Mrs Champernowne that I am quite recovered from my 'chill'. The old buzzard may be suspicious and make mean comments about it being little short of a miracle, but I cannot miss a meal. I have a long night ahead of me.

Just after noon, Ellie and Masou slipped into my chamber giggling and with their arms full of clothes. At once I could see that these garments had never been near a spit boy.

'I got them from our costume trunk,' explained Masou, who was dressed in bright breeches, jerkin and cloak.

Ellie held out a full skirt, decorated with ribbons and bells like Masou's costume. There was a short jacket to match, made of a bright but tatty velvet. I was going to feel much warmer as a pedlar than as a spit boy.

I went behind the screen in the corner of my bedchamber and slipped the clothes on over my kirtle, then put on my riding boots, still muddy from the night before. It was lucky that I had forgotten to put them out for Olwen. 'I'm ready!' I said, giving a twirl in my borrowed clothes.

Masou plonked a large floppy hat adorned with three bright feathers on my head.

I stood in the middle of the chamber and struck a pose. 'Who will buy my fine wares?'

'That's no good,' laughed Ellie. 'You sound like the Queen herself. No one's going to believe you're a pedlar if you talk in your fancy Court voice.'

'I hadn't thought of that!' I grinned. 'How should I talk then?'

'Like me,' said Ellie.

I tried again. 'Oo will bouy mee faine weirs? How is that?'

Ellie fell back on the bed and Masou held his sides as they howled with laughter.

'What's wrong with that?' I demanded. 'I sounded just like you, didn't I, Ellie?'

'You sounded more like you've swallowed your tongue!' Ellie gasped, wiping her eyes on her sleeve.

I tried again. 'How woll bay mai feen wars!'

'Now you sound like a halfwit who has swallowed her tongue!' Masou chortled. 'Stop, else I shall split my sides!'

'Then I shall not speak at all!' I said crossly, expecting them to tell me it was all a jest. To my horror, they looked relieved.

'You have it, Grace!' exclaimed Masou. 'We will say that you cannot speak for you are a tongue-tied halfwit. Think of it – for once I will get to do all the talking with no inter-ruptions from my lady.'

I tried to fix him with a haughty look but he just grinned and, whipping a little pot from his pocket, began to smear charcoal on my face.

'I borrowed this from the fire,' he laughed. 'Now you are a *dirty* tongue-tied halfwit!'

I caught sight of myself in Lady Sarah's looking glass. He was right. Even the Queen wouldn't recognize me. I waved my arms, waggled my head from side to side and made mumbling noises.

'No different from the Lady Grace we know and love!' declared Masou as Ellie giggled at my antics.

'Beware!' I warned them. 'It is lucky for you that we have no time, or the Lady Grace you know and love would clout you both! Now, we are dressed as pedlars but what are we to sell? I have a few sweets left over from the Frost Fair, but that is not enough.'

'I have thought of that,' said Masou, and he tipped out a sackful of ribbons and buttons and fancy lengths of lace. 'These I found in the tumblers' costume trunk. They will not be missed.' He put them back in the sack. 'But we must sell them from the bag for there were no pedlars' trays in our trunk.'

I was just adding the ribbon sweets to the wares when Ellie's hand shot out, pinched one and stuffed it in her mouth.

'Just making sure they taste good,' she mumbled, grinning. 'Now, begone. We can't have no pedlars in ladies' bedchambers!' And she shooed us out.

Masou and I covered our gaudy clothes in long, heavy cloaks, and I put on my mask, for it would go very hard for two pedlars found within Whitehall. The Queen's Guard can be very quick with their swords and may not ask questions first.

The frozen Thames was as busy as ever as people made their way to and from the Frost Fair. We set off away from the fair, upstream towards Westminster. I found it quite easy walking on the ice, but I wished I could have skated again.

Soon Masou had attracted a following of children as he capered across the ice, playing a jolly tune on a pipe, like the Pied Piper of Hamelin Town. That left me to carry the sack – and now it had our cloaks and my mask in as well!

By the time we'd reached Will Stubbs's cottage we had quite a crowd, young and old. Whenever Masou performs at Court, everyone looks at him – and here it was no different. All the children wanted to talk to him. They pestered him with requests to teach them how to juggle and shrieked with delight when he produced eggs from their ears.

I stayed in the background, mumbling now and again and trying to listen carefully to their excited chatter.

'Welcome, all,' exclaimed Masou with a deep bow. 'We are poor pedlars, here to entertain and sell our wares. I will show you the fine art of juggling while my sister here – you must forgive her for she is a dullard – will show you our wares. Be not afraid, she is harmless but tongue-tied, so ask not the price for everything is but a halfpenny.'

I thumped Masou with the sack, which made everyone laugh. Then, mumbling, I wandered around the crowd showing what we had to sell.

Masou plucked caps from the heads of some nearby children and began to juggle with them.

'Where you from, Master Pedlar?' asked a woman in the crowd.

'We hail from the south, where the sun burnishes the skin and oranges ripen on the trees, even in the winter,' Masou replied, not taking his eyes off the hats.

'Why ain't your sister dark like you?' shouted someone else.

'She is afeard of the sun and hides away from it,' answered Masou cheerily. 'Yet we are not accustomed to such cold and have never seen frozen water like this before. What is it?'

'Why, it is the river Thames,' giggled a young boy.

'No!' gasped Masou, clapping his hands dramatically to his heart and dropping all the hats. 'Not the great river Thames? Surely it will soon break through this frosty harness?' Then he began to leap about as if he were scared the ice would crack beneath him. The crowd loved it. 'Tell me more of this frozen water,' he called, flicking the caps back onto each head. 'What boats sail on it?'

The children screeched with laughter.

'Boats don't sail on ice,' explained a small grubby girl. 'You need sleds.'

'Sleds, is it?' asked Masou. He cupped his chin in one hand thoughtfully. 'And are they good sport?'

'Oh yes,' said his young informant, 'and we makes skates out of pieces of wood and bone and we skids about all over the place.'

I stopped handing out my wares and went to stand by my 'pedlar brother'. When I counted I found we had earned sixpence half-penny for our efforts − although, if I am to be honest, I think it was Masou's antics that earned us the money. The grown-ups began to drift away but the children all stayed, fascinated by their southern visitors.

'And doth the sun not melt the ice?' Masou wanted to know.

'No! 'Tis too thick for that.' This came as a chorus from all the children.

'But what about the moon?' Masou had a twinkle in his eye. 'Doth the moon not melt it at night?'

The children shook their heads solemnly.

The grubby little girl shuddered. 'It's scary after dark. The river makes horrible creaking noises. No one goes out on the ice at night.'

'Harry Stubbs the waterman does!' piped up an older boy. I felt Masou stiffen beside me as the boy carried on, 'Me mam says he goes out nigh on every night. He's been making runs on the ice using a sled. We don't know where he goes, but late it is, just after the ten o'clock curfew. And no one's meant to go out after the curfew bell sounds!'

Masou suddenly stepped back, spun round on the ice and did a somersault in the air, to the delight of his audience. 'We must journey on, my friends,' he declared, 'along this frozen river Thames of yours. You have been a fine audience and we will always remember you, our Children of the Ice.' And he swept them a deep bow.

I did a clumsy curtsy and mumbled a bit, which made them all titter. Then we set off back towards Whitehall in the fading light.

I was desperate to speak and found it hard to wait until we were out of hearing distance.

'So the dead man's brother goes out on strange missions at night,' I said as soon as I could. 'That sounds most suspicious. Mayhap there is some connection between these midnight errands and Will Stubbs's murder. I believe we have a lead at last.'

'We must find out where he journeys to,' said Masou.

When we got back to Whitehall we sought out Ellie. She was in the starching room, attending to a ruff by the poor light of a flickering tallow candle.

Throwing our cloaks off, we excitedly told her what we had discovered, jabbering away and forgetting we were still dressed as pedlars.

I showed Ellie the coins we had earned and slipped them into her pocket. Her face lit up. I felt pleased that I had given the money to her, but also chastened because what had seemed such a paltry sum to me was obviously riches to Ellie.

'What are we going to do now?' she asked, pushing the ruff aside.

'I'm going to follow Harry the waterman and see what he's up to,' I declared. 'Tonight!'

Ellie looked horrified. 'Not on your own

you're not!' she said severely. 'That man might have had something to do with his own brother's murder! Me and Masou are coming with you.'

'I don't want to get you into trouble,' I insisted. 'If we are caught by the City watchmen it could go badly for you both – for we shall be out after curfew.'

'Oh, Grace,' said Ellie. 'You've been listening to tales of the past. We'll likely not even see a watchman. Nowadays folk are not so bothered about curfew. I shouldn't think the City will even be locked up. So we'll be with you, and no argument – won't we, Masou?'

'Allah be praised! What joy! I shall have frozen toes once more!' exclaimed Masou, rolling his eyes. 'Still, I shall have no trouble slipping out tonight, for my lord the Earl of Leicester is back at Court and the Queen has ordered a private dinner with her favourite.'

'In that case the Queen will not notice my absence,' I told them. Then a thought occurred to me. 'But I mean to skate. How can you keep up?'

'It's not just Maids of Honour what can skate, my fine lady!' laughed Ellie. 'Anyone can strap a length of bone to their boot.'

'Especially if it be carved and shaped by an expert,' boasted Masou, tapping his own chest.

'Very well,' I agreed, secretly pleased not to be venturing out on the ice on my own at night. 'Then we shall meet down here when the clock chimes nine—'

'What's all this?' came a screech, and Mrs Fadget suddenly appeared in the gloomy room. She took one look at our pedlar clothes and started waving her arms madly. 'Cut-throats! Thieves!' she shrieked. 'We'll all be murdered in our beds. Help! Ellie, fetch a broom!'

Before I could say anything, Masou grabbed my hand and pulled me towards the door. 'Pray pardon, mistress,' he said. 'We are simply trying to sell our wares. No harm meant.' He grinned mischievously. 'My sister begs pardon too, but cannot say it for she is a tongue-tied halfwit. *Ow!*' This last was addressed to my boot, which had made its acquaintance with his shin.

I was enjoying the sight of the odious Mrs Fadget in a panic, but I knew that any moment now her screeching would alert the guard and my secret investigations wouldn't be as secret as I would wish.

'Mrs Fadget!' I said sternly. 'Stop that noise. Do you not recognize one of Her Majesty's Maids of Honour? Masou and I are merely trying costumes for a masque for Her Majesty. What would she say if she heard you?'

Mrs Fadget stared hard at my face. 'Oh, my lady!' she gasped as she recognized me. 'Forgive me.' She scuttled past us and disappeared. I do not believe I have ever seen such a big grin on Ellie's face!

So now I am getting ready for a quiet supper with Mrs Champernowne and the other Maids of Honour. I will eat my fill and then, alas, I will suffer a relapse of my chill and 'retire early for the night', for I must be away from the palace and at Westminster well before ten of the clock. My heart thuds in my chest, but whether it is from excitement or fear I know not.

The Twenty-eighth Day of November, in the Year of Our Lord 1569

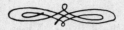

Late afternoon

I am sitting in the Queen's bedchamber, by a roaring fire, wrapped in Her Majesty's best mink cloak! I have sweetmeats and a cinnamon posset at my side, and the Queen has given fierce orders that we are not to be disturbed. She is dictating a letter to one of her secretaries and looking over at me from time to time to see how I am faring. I am in truth far too hot, but dare not offend Her Majesty by throwing off the cloak, when she has tucked it round me with her own hand. I have already had to plead with her to let me write in my daybooke for I must retell my adventure of last night. Hell's teeth! I must also take care not to spill ink on Her Majesty's fine mink.

I pray I have enough ink to make this entry,

for I have so much to tell! I have slept much of the day and I hope my wits are not too befuddled to make a good record of what has happened.

As soon as I had supped last night, I excused myself, saying I felt feeble with the chill again. To help the pretence I had put some of Lady Sarah's white lead on my cheeks before I came down.

'What did I tell you, Grace?' said Mrs Champernowne crossly, leading me off to my bed. 'You were up too hastily, look you. Have you a sore throat?'

I shook my head quickly and said no, it was just the shivers. Mrs Champernowne would be only too happy to hunt down a spider – for me to swallow as a cure – if I'd said yes.

It was lucky that the Queen was having a private meal with my Lord of Leicester or she would have called for my Uncle Cavendish to physic me. I couldn't tell Her Majesty that I was intending to leave the palace and follow a suspicious waterman along the moonlit ice. She would have forbidden it out of hand.

As soon as Mrs Champernowne had gone, I threw off my gown and sleeves, and pulled on my old green woollen kirtle, hat, gloves and a good warm cloak. I could not risk a newer garment becoming torn or muddied and questions being asked.

Grabbing my skates, I made my way through one of Masou's secret ways, down to the heavy oak door that leads to the Privy Bridge landing stage. I heard a distant clock strike nine and I hoped Masou and Ellie would be waiting.

As I closed the door behind me, two shadows pulled away from the gloom and for a moment my heart thumped alarmingly, until I realized it was indeed my two friends. They both looked as if they were wearing many layers of clothes. I didn't ask where they'd got them from.

'Did you have any trouble getting away?' I whispered.

'No,' Masou whispered back. 'I asked Mr Somers if I might be excused as the Queen is having her private supper and should not want much entertainment. I believe he thinks I am off to meet some young lady. It would surprise him greatly to find it was actually two!'

Ellie giggled and quickly clapped her hand over her mouth to stop the noise.

We made our way down onto the ice, strapped on our skates and set off, trying to make as little sound as possible. I thought the Palace Guard might be about, for Whitehall is always watched, even on the coldest of nights – though Masou said they were more likely to be found round a fire with their ale than round the palace walls with their swords. Even so, we kept as close to the shadowy bank as we could. Ellie and Masou were able skaters. I am sure it was because of the fine skates that Masou had fashioned.

It was difficult to see, until the moon came out from behind a cloud and lit the Thames. In the silence of the night, we could hear the ice creak eerily as the river flowed beneath it.

We stopped a little way from the Stubbses' cottage and climbed up onto the bank, where we hid behind the low wall of the pigsty. It was bitterly cold and we huddled together for what seemed like ages.

'Can't we go in with the pig?' asked Ellie, her teeth chattering.

'What about the smell?' I said.

'The pig will just have to get used to it!' whispered Masou.

I was about to pinch him when, at last, we heard a latch creak and the door of the cottage open. The light of a lantern spilled out onto the frosty ground and we could see the silhouette of a heavy-set man.

'Where you going?' came a woman's voice. 'You're never home. It's the same every night.'

'None of your business, wife!' snarled the man. I recognized that voice. It was Harry the waterman. 'Now shut the door and think no more on it.' And with that he strode straight towards us!

We ducked our heads down and lay there, not daring to move a muscle. If Harry came round the pigsty he would see us. The footsteps were getting nearer and it was too late to take to our heels. Then we heard him fling the sty gate open and go inside. He came out again, dragging something behind him.

I dared to peek round the wall of the sty. Harry was making his way towards the bank, towing a sled behind him.

'Quick,' I whispered. 'We must follow him.'

'Not too close, Grace,' hissed Masou, 'or he will hear us.'

Harry's lantern cast a glow over the ice around him as he marched along pulling his sled. We followed, keeping close to the mounds of ice by the bank.

'We must stay well back,' hissed Masou, pulling us to hide behind a boat stuck in the ice, 'else if Harry Stubbs turns to look, we shall be as visible as a camel at a banquet!'

'Suppose he hears our skates?' said Ellie in a worried whisper.

'No fear of that,' replied Masou. 'Allah himself would not hear us over the noise of that sled.'

We waited until Harry Stubbs was well ahead, and then made a quick dash to hide under the landing stage at Star Chamber. Then we followed again.

When we reached Temple Steps, the water-man was already disappearing amongst the empty booths of the Frost Fair.

'Faster!' I urged my friends. 'We mustn't lose him.'

We darted between the dark, shadowy stalls, stopping now and again to listen for sounds of the sled. It was very strange to see the fair so eerie and silent when it had been so bustling during the day. Then, suddenly, we came out onto clear ice again and there he was, not twenty paces ahead. All he had to do was turn and he would discover us!

I stopped so suddenly that Ellie cannoned into me and I fell forwards onto my hands and knees. Masou and Ellie flattened themselves on the ice next to me as Harry Stubbs stopped, raised his lantern and looked around suspiciously. Luckily for us, a cloud had covered the moon and we must have been invisible to him, for after a while he turned and walked on.

'That was close,' I breathed.

'And cold!' moaned Masou, as we lay there, not daring to get up. 'If you persist in being the Queen's Lady Pursuivant, prithee do it in a warmer season.'

'I shall tell all miscreants that only summer crimes will be permitted in future!' I retorted. 'Now, let him go a little further, then we'll follow.'

'He seems to be heading for the bank,' said Ellie, pointing, 'right by London Bridge.'

Harry took his sled as near to the bridge as he could. We watched as he hid it amongst some frozen driftwood. Then he pulled himself up onto a landing stage close to the bridge and set off into the darkness.

We scrambled to our feet and skated as fast as we could to the bank.

'Is he making for the heart of the City?' asked Ellie excitedly, as we clambered onto the landing stage and pulled off our skates.

Masou stowed our skates in a leather bag that was tied to his back with a long leather strap, and we followed the light of the lantern down a dark alley.

'Oh, Grace, do you think we're near where they've been making the counterfeit coins?' Ellie wondered.

'I hope so, Ellie,' I said. 'I pray we're not following another false lead.'

'Indeed,' said Masou in a grave and mysterious voice. 'Harry Stubbs could be murderer of his own kin! In which case, what would he do to three strangers like our selves?'

'I wish you hadn't said that,' whimpered Ellie, looking round fearfully.

We followed Harry Stubbs as he wove his way through the shadowy streets. These were routes I had never followed on horseback or by litter, and Ellie and Masou seemed to have no more inkling of where we were than I did. Masou took hold of our sleeves to keep us together and I was glad of it.

It seemed darker than ever now, for the ramshackle dwellings were very close together and seemed to be toppling forwards until they almost touched over our heads. It did not look like a friendly neighbourhood.

Ellie must have been thinking the same. She shuddered as she looked up. 'I reckon the sun never makes its way down here,' she whispered.

The houses were dark and shuttered. Only now and then did we glimpse the brief light of a candle. It was by Harry's flickering lantern ahead of us that we kept him in sight.

'It is so quiet,' murmured Masou, pulling even more tightly on my sleeve. 'It could be the city of the dead!'

'Don't say things like that!' I hissed, giving him a pinch. And then I heard a strange scrabbling noise. I froze and pulled at Masou's sleeve. 'Did you hear that?' I muttered out of the corner of my mouth.

We all stood as still as statues.

Suddenly, there was the most awful wailing and a black creature landed on Masou's shoulders!

'Allah save me!' Masou gasped, flailing at it with both hands.

With another unearthly cry, the shadowy creature jumped to the ground and sped off into the darkness.

Ellie stifled a nervous giggle. 'It was only a cat,' she said. 'It slipped off that roof!'

We clutched each other's sleeves, weak in

our relief. But when we looked around for Harry's light, it had gone.

'He must have turned a corner,' I said.

We scampered and skidded along the icy cobbles. The path — it was now too narrow to be called a street — bent round a decaying old warehouse and turned into a dank, dismal alley. There was no sign of the waterman.

'I think we've lost him,' panted Ellie.

'No,' I gasped, pointing into the distance. 'Look!'

At the far end of the alley we could just make out a tiny bobbing light.

We ran as silently as we could towards it. As we got closer we could see the heavy figure of Harry Stubbs and the glint of the river Thames beyond him.

'Heaven be praised!' breathed Ellie.

'Has he led us around in a circle?' asked Masou.

'No, we must be east of London Bridge,' I whispered as we stopped in the shelter of the last tumbledown house before the riverbank. 'See, the water isn't frozen this side of its arches.'

We crept nearer. Indeed, the river was flowing and taking great slabs of ice downstream.

Harry was clambering into a small rowing boat. He pushed off downriver with the oars.

'What are we going to do now?' I said anxiously. 'We cannot follow him without a boat.'

'There may be one down by the water's edge,' said Masou.

We ran to the bank. Masou was right: there were several small boats tied up to a jetty, bobbing in the inky black water. We were just peering into one when we heard shuffling footsteps behind us.

''Ere!' came a shout. 'You trying to steal one of my fine craft?'

I was so scared I jumped and nearly toppled into the river.

We turned to find a wizened old man, holding up a lantern that barely cast a light.

'These are my boats,' he said. 'Well, in a manner of speaking. I looks after them for the owners, like.'

Masou gave him a small bow. 'We would

never think of such a heinous crime as theft, kind sir,' he said. 'But we are desirous of venturing upon the river and are in need of a stout craft.'

The man looked him up and down. 'What foreign talk is that?' he demanded.

Ellie went right up to the old man. 'Listen 'ere,' she said loudly. 'We want to hire a boat and we've got money!'

At the mention of money the old man's face changed as if he'd taken off a mask.

I looked at Masou in dismay. I had not thought to bring any money. But Ellie fumbled in her bodice and proudly brought out the coins Masou and I had given her.

'That all?' scoffed the old man, pocketing the coins in a hurry. 'You can have the one at the end. And mind you bring it back.'

'I will replace your coins,' I promised Ellie as we raced along the jetty and scrambled into the tiny battered old boat that was moored at the end.

Masou and Ellie took an oar each. I kneeled at the prow, for the boat was so small we only just fitted in. At least from here I could be the lookout.

As we pushed away from the bank, I peered across the murky water to see if there was any sign of Harry's light. Suddenly, I found myself facing London Bridge, and I wished I wasn't, for I caught sight of the pikes on the southern edge sporting their traitors' heads. I had seen them many a time during the day, but at night their silhouettes filled me with horror.

'We're going the wrong way,' I exclaimed.

'Ellie's work in the laundry has given her a man's muscles,' complained Masou. 'She's pulling too hard on her oar.'

'Then you pull harder on yourn,' Ellie told him, 'before I clout you with mine.'

At last we managed to put London Bridge behind us and began to make progress across the water. I had no idea where we should be heading. We rowed on downriver, passing tall ships moored midstream. There were muffled thumps as their hulls were buffeted by blocks of ice, and we had to take pains to avoid being hit ourselves. Now and then I could see lights flickering on the northern bank, but none turned out to be Harry Stubbs with his lantern.

'We've lost him again!' I cried.

At that moment the Tower loomed up before us. It seemed an age since I'd come here with Sir Edward Latimer to see how the mint worked, yet it was only two days ago. As we rowed past I heard an eleven o'clock bell tolling. I looked desperately up and down the river, but I couldn't see much, for the moon was behind a cloud.

'If we don't find him soon we'll have to turn back,' said Ellie, laying down her oar. 'We can't row all night. We'll freeze to death and they'll be laying coins on *our* eyes.'

'Just a few yards further,' I pleaded. 'I feel in my bones that Harry must have something to do with the counterfeiting. If only we could find out where he is.'

'Quiet!' whispered Masou. 'What was that?'

Across the water came the distant sound of a low whistle.

'It's coming from the Tower!' exclaimed Ellie.

She and Masou pulled gently on the oars and we made for the Water Gate.

As we neared the high wooden wharf we could see a small boat moored there. And on the bench was Harry's lantern.

'He's here somewhere,' I whispered.

We tied our boat to a little ladder. Masou held it steady as I pulled myself up the slippery rungs to the top of the ladder and peered over.

'Can you see anything?' hissed Ellie. The ladder wobbled alarmingly as she struggled up to join me.

We could just make out Harry standing by the moat in front of the Tower. He looked up at the battlements and we heard another low whistle.

'Sir Edward has lodgings in the Tower,' I whispered to Ellie. 'If he were a braver sort of man we could try to get his help.'

'He's probably quivering under his bed-clothes at this very minute,' said Ellie. 'You said he's even afeard of the bell.' Then she grabbed my arm. 'There's a window opening above, Grace,' she hissed. 'And there's some-one there!'

I looked up at a faintly lit window in the battlements. And my heart skipped a beat, because there, at the window, was the shape of a man – and he was pointing a bow and arrow straight at us!

Ellie tried to pull me down, but I couldn't move a muscle – just as a mouse must feel when cornered by a cat. I watched in a trance as the man pulled back the bowstring and let the arrow fly. It sped towards us over the moat and thud-ded into a bollard not three yards from our heads.

'Get down, Grace, before he tries again!' hissed Ellie, shaking me out of my trance. 'We've got to get away!'

'Wait,' I whispered back. I had noticed something. 'He hasn't even seen us. We're well hidden here. The arrow wasn't meant for us. There's a rope attached to it.'

Harry strode over to the arrow, pulled the rope free and tied it quickly to the bollard. He threw the arrow into the river and gave the rope a tug.

Up at the window his accomplice hung two sacks over the rope, one on either side, and let go. The sacks slid down into the waiting arms of the waterman. They must have been heavy for he grunted as he caught them. He put them down on the wharf, and as he did so, I heard the chink of coins.

'Did you hear that?' I whispered to Ellie.

She nodded. 'I think we've found our counterfeiters!' she breathed.

Harry untied the rope. The figure up above swiftly pulled it back in and silently shut the window.

'Quick!' I hissed to Ellie. 'Back to our boat.'

There was a nasty moment as we both tried to clamber back into the boat at the same time. It wobbled on the water as if it would over-turn, and it took all Masou's strength to steady it. Luckily we were well hidden by the wharf.

We stayed close to the wooden stanchions and waited until we saw Harry rowing back in the direction of London Bridge.

As we followed, keeping a good distance behind, Ellie told Masou what we'd seen. 'He must have got counterfeit coins right there in his sacks,' she said excitedly.

'So there never was another mint set up!' I put in. 'Whoever is employing Harry must be using the Royal Mint to make his counterfeit coins, right under the noses of the mint workers!'

'And then the waterman comes for them at dead of night,' said Masou, pulling hard on his oar.

'Are we to go back now, Grace, and tell the Queen?' Ellie said hopefully. She looked frozen to the marrow.

'No,' I said firmly, trying to keep the boat and its lantern in sight. 'We must follow Harry back to his sled and see where he delivers the coins.'

'By Allah, this rowing gets harder!' exclaimed Masou.

'That's probably because we're going against the tide,' puffed Ellie.

I suddenly realized that my feet were getting very cold . . . and wet. 'The boat's leaking!' I gasped. I could find nothing to use to bail out the icy water so I had to pull off my gloves and make do with my cupped hands. It was not easy as I was so cramped. 'Can't you row any faster?' I urged. 'I am losing all feeling in my fingers and Harry's almost out of sight!'

'By Shaitan!' muttered Masou. 'We are rowing like galley slaves as it is.'

'The water's up to my ankles!' yelped Ellie. 'Bail harder, Grace!'

'I can't!' I wailed. 'The river is winning! You must make for the bank. We'll have to do the rest on foot. If we haven't lost him, that is.'

With great difficulty, Masou and Ellie swung the boat round and we headed for the shore. The water was beginning to lap over the gunwales now and it looked as if we were going to sink. I could feel the freezing water slopping in my boots.

Then, as we drew near to a landing stage, Masou stood up in the boat and grabbed at the wooden struts. 'Make haste, ladies!' he said. 'Climb onto here.'

We did as he said, and clung fast to the side of the stage, our feet slipping on the slimy wooden supports underneath us. My kirtle and cloak felt as heavy as lead as I pulled myself out of the boat. Ellie was soon by my side. We turned and saw the rowing boat slowly disappearing into the dark water.

'Where's Masou?' cried Ellie in alarm.

'Here,' came a voice from above our heads.

Masou was already on the stage and holding out his hands to help us up. We crept – or rather, squelched – along the landing stage to the wharf, making sure we avoided the old man who had hired us the boat. Ellie was all for going to demand her coins back, so we had to drag her along the quayside.

'Which way now?' I asked as we peered into the dark, gloomy streets.

'I see the lantern!' exclaimed Masou. 'A little way up yonder.'

'I thought he'd be well away by now,' said Ellie, wringing out her wet skirts.

'Don't forget he is burdened down with the false coins,' Masou reminded her. 'He cannot move too quickly.'

We followed him back to the west side of

the bridge and sheltered behind a buttress, putting on our skates, while Harry got his sled out of its hiding place and loaded the sacks on.

His pace across the ice was much slower. Now we needed to hang back, for the moon was free of cloud and the Thames well lit.

'Where is he going?' muttered Masou. It was the question I am sure we were all wondering.

'Back to his cottage?' Ellie suggested.

'I don't think so,' I told her. 'Remember he has been making runs night after night. There must be quite a hoard of coins by now. It would be hard to hide all that from the widow Stubbs and her children.'

'And even his wife didn't seem to know what he was about,' added Ellie.

'The freeze must have made the counter-feiters change their plans,' I said, banging my poor frozen hands together. 'Harry must have used his boat before the river froze – and then had to quickly make a sled.' I reflected that Harry must be brave indeed to regularly shoot down London Bridge, for the river flows very fast as it spills through the arches of the bridge, and it takes great skill and courage to take a boat through those rapids.

'He scares me!' exclaimed Ellie.

Masou suddenly grasped my arm. 'He's changing course!'

The waterman had gone past Temple Steps and was now heading for some stone stairs beyond.

We hung back while he unloaded the sled, lifted the sacks onto his shoulders and climbed up the stairs to a huge wall. He pushed open a door in the wall and disappeared inside.

We skated over to the stairs. I tried to get my bearings in the moonlight. 'I think this must be one of the large houses in the Strand,' I said. 'All their grounds run down to the river and they each have a landing stage.'

We took off our skates, shoved them in Masou's bag and climbed the slippery steps.

Further along the bank there was an ornate iron gate in the wall. I recognized it. 'I'm right,' I whispered, 'for beyond that gate is

Somerset House, which belongs to the Queen, and I know that to be on the Strand.' I had been there once for a masque – we had travelled from Hampton Court by royal barge. 'I have no idea who lives here,' I added. 'But it could be the leader of the counterfeiters. And there is only one way to find out.'

I pushed open the door in the wall and we slipped inside to find ourselves in a knot garden, which was overgrown and covered in unswept leaves. I marched up to the huge carved door of the house and raised my hand to the knocker.

Masou caught my arm and held it firmly. 'You cannot go up to a grand house at this time of night, looking so dishevelled and talking in your fine voice without arousing suspicion,' he said with a grin. 'Mayhap 'tis another chance for you to be a tongue-tied halfwit – for you do it so well, Grace.'

He moved on before I had a chance to give him a clever reply. It was as well – I couldn't think of one just then.

'We shall go to the kitchen door and I shall beg for alms,' he told us.

'But begging's unlawful!' gasped Ellie. 'We'll be thrown into Bridewell.'

'Not us,' said Masou. 'We're too nimble on our feet to end up in prison. At the first sniff of trouble we'll run!'

So the three of us went round the side of the house, past many windows, all in darkness, and up to the kitchen door. Masou knocked loudly.

The door was opened by a thin youth holding a candle. He looked familiar to me but I couldn't place where I knew him from.

'Greetings, fine sir,' said Masou, putting on a feeble voice. 'We are poor folk and are come to beg a favour of the master of this house. Tell me, who is your master?'

The boy puffed out his chest. 'Why, I am in the service of—'

At this moment Harry Stubbs appeared. He pushed past the boy to take his leave.

I stepped back quickly to keep my face hidden in the shadows.

'What's going on here?' he asked suspiciously, seeing Masou, Ellie and me on the doorstep.

'Beggars,' answered the boy.

'None of my business then,' said Harry roughly.

He was about to go past without a word, when his lantern lit my face. 'I know you!' he growled. 'I know you from somewhere.' He thrust his horrible, unshaven face close to mine.

I could smell the onions he'd had for his dinner and I'll warrant his teeth had never seen a toothcloth.

Masou began to step backwards, pulling Ellie and me with him. 'No, good sir, you are mistaken. We are strangers to this city.'

'I know who you are!' roared Harry, jabbing a finger in my direction. 'You're that meddling Maid from the palace who came asking questions about my brother!' He reached out to grab at me, but Masou and Ellie got in his way.

'Run, Grace!' yelled Masou.

I turned to make a dash for it, but the young

boy was too quick for me. He caught me, pinned my arms behind my back and dragged me back to the door and into the hall beyond. I yelled and squirmed in his grasp but he was stronger than he looked.

Harry had Masou and Ellie tightly grasped in his huge hands. He pulled them inside too, then kicked the door shut with a thump. 'Come on, Sam,' he growled. 'We'll get these little spies shut up and deal with them later. Not a word to the master when 'e gets here, mind. 'E won't want to hear there's been trouble.'

We were dragged along the passageway, through a kitchen where a feeble fire glowed in a grate and up a creaky old spiral staircase. Then we were taken into a chamber and thrown into a large closet. We heard a key turn in the lock. Footsteps faded away, and then there was silence.

It was dark as pitch. We lay in a pile, sore and battered from our manhandling. I think I had it the worst for I was underneath, and lying on something hard. 'What are we going to do?' I said, trying to keep the despair out of my voice. I wished I could get to my feet.

'I dunno,' came Ellie's voice. It sounded bleak.

Masou was muttering to himself.

'Stop fidgeting, you silly boy!' groaned Ellie. 'Let me get up. You may not be able to see it, but that was me eye you nearly poked out!'

'Forgive me, sweet Ellie,' I heard Masou say calmly, 'but I nearly have it— Yes!'

There was a flash and a small light appeared.

'It is always wise to travel with a tinder box and a candle!' announced Masou smugly. It wasn't the brightest of lights but it felt as if the sun had come out.

Masou held the candle stub up with one hand and helped me to my feet with the other.

We looked around at the inside of our tiny prison. The floor was covered in sacks. Some had fallen open, and in the candlelight we could see the gleam of silver coins!

I scooped up a handful and examined them closely. 'These look identical to the ones placed on Will Stubbs's eyes,' I exclaimed, throwing them down. 'I think we have found the counterfeit coins. And if by chance they are genuine, then they are the Queen's new design and they should certainly be at the Tower.'

'But the counterfeiters have found us!' said Ellie grimly. 'And their master will be at the house soon.'

'We must escape and get back to Court straight away,' I decided, 'and without the villains knowing. If we can lead Mr Hatton and the Gentlemen of the Queen's Guard back here in time, they can catch the miscreants and their master red-handed. But how are we going to get out of this prison? Ouch! That was my foot you just trod on, Masou. What are you doing?'

Masou was fidgeting again. 'I am working on our escape,' he said with a grin. He fiddled in his pocket and triumphantly produced a thin, pointed bone. 'This is my toothpick. The Queen ate swan last night, and the leftovers were the devil for my teeth. But I had not thought I would have need of the toothpick again so soon.'

I leaned over and watched as he inserted the

bone into the lock. 'You are clever, Masou,' I said.

'I know,' he agreed. 'It is a gift. Now hold the candle stub up for me and we shall be out of here before you can say silver sixpence!'

I did as he asked.

He wriggled the bone in the lock but nothing happened.

'So what's your next great idea, O Gifted One?' demanded Ellie. 'Whatever it is, make it soon – they could be back at any minute.'

'Patience!' hissed Masou. He gave the bone another twist.

'Something went click! You're getting there!' I exclaimed.

'Shh!' ordered Masou. 'I need to listen.'

There was a small rasping sound from the lock. Then a loud clunk. We all held our breath, hoping no one in the house had heard.

Masou gently pushed the door and it swung open. He cautiously peered out. 'Follow me,' he whispered.

We crept out and into the chamber. It was lit only by the moonlight filtering in through the windowpanes.

Masou held up his spluttering candle, making our shadows move eerily on the walls. The room was bare of furniture and smelled damp and musty.

'This is most strange,' I hissed. 'I believed these houses to be owned by the wealthy, yet I could think this was the house of a pauper. Look at the peeling wallpaper – and not a portrait in sight.' My mind was racing. Whose house could this possibly be? Who was the master Harry Stubbs had spoken of?

I peeped out through the dirty window. I could just make out the knot garden. We were two storeys above it. There would be no climbing out and escaping from here. 'We must get downstairs,' I said. 'But not the way we came up. It would be too creaky and give us away.'

In single file we slowly made our way towards an open gallery. Here there was a large stone staircase. We stopped and listened, but it seemed that, apart from the kitchen, the house was as good as empty and we reached the bottom of the two flights undetected. We found ourselves in the dark entrance hall. It was hung with cobwebs and there were no rushes or sweet herbs on the tiled floor, and no furnishings save for a battered old chest. We could see chambers on either side of the hall and the huge carved door ahead of us.

'Not that way,' whispered Masou. 'It could be guarded. There must be a window to the side of the house.' He moved towards the chamber on the left, silent as a cat.

Ellie and I started to follow when we heard footsteps approaching. Masou snuffed out his light and darted away through the doorway. I pulled Ellie down behind the chest with me. I felt myself shivering, and I don't think it was just the cold. I peeked round the edge of the chest.

The shadowy figures of three men came into view. The first held a candle and strode angrily along, while the second, a much larger man, was dragging a third bound figure behind him. They stopped close to us. Now I could see their faces in the flickering candlelight and I felt relief suddenly flood over me. The man with the candle was Sir Edward Latimer!

Somehow he must have found out about the counterfeiters already, for his prisoner was Harry Stubbs, squirming in the grip of Sir Edward's burly bodyguard.

I must have misjudged Sir Edward, I thought, for this was no milksop who cringed under bedclothes and went faint at the mention of a dead body. This was a man who had foiled a counterfeiter's plot and that took some bravery!

I was about to leave my hiding place and tell him about the money upstairs in the cupboard when he spoke.

'Bring the fool here, Tyler!' he said.

There was something in his manner that made me hesitate. His voice was harsh and cruel and almost unrecognizable. I didn't move.

The bodyguard pushed Harry forwards so roughly that he fell onto the tiles.

'You miserable dolt, Stubbs!' growled Sir Edward, giving him a vicious kick which made him groan. 'Your blundering has put me in danger. It is lucky the boy told me of our un-invited guests, for you would have kept your

carelessness a secret from me. Do you not understand the meaning of secrecy? The counterfeit
money was supposed to be kept hidden until it
was time to release it amongst the Queen's
genuine new coins. But thanks to you I might
as well have shouted my doings from St Paul's
tower for all to hear! You have failed me from
start to finish. I should have got rid of you after
you let slip to your brother what we were doing.
'Tis a pity my arrow this night struck the bollard
and not your cowardly chest.'

My mind reeled. Sir Edward had shot the
arrow from the Tower, and lowered the sacks
of coins to Harry Stubbs! I could hardly believe
it, but Sir Edward, the Mint Warden himself,
was the villain behind the counterfeiting.
Clearly his dandified ways and girlish manners
were nothing but an act – but a very convin-
cing act it had been!

'I never meant to tell my brother anything,'
Harry was whining. He was pale and sweat-
ing. 'Will found a coin and asked me what it
was all about. I told him to mind his own business, I swear.'

'I don't believe you,' snarled Sir Edward, grinding his heel into Harry's fingers and making him howl with pain. 'He came to me and announced that the two of you wanted nothing more to do with my scheme.'

'And 'e's having nothing more to do with it now,' sniggered the bodyguard. 'I saw to that.'

I could hear Ellie's frightened breathing next to me. I was surprised that no one else could.

Sir Edward turned and struck his servant across the mouth. 'Stow you, Tyler! You have served me no better. You were supposed to leave the boat where only *Harry* would find his brother's body. Only *he* was to see the coins on Will Stubbs's dead eyes – and thus know that there would be no backing out.'

Tyler shuffled and bobbed his head. 'I'm sorry, my lord,' he muttered, rubbing his cheek. 'I did strangle him like you told me, and put him in his own boat and moor it by his cottage. 'Twasn't my fault the boat floated off.'

Sir Edward seemed to grow taller in his rage. 'Then whose fault was it? Jack Frost's? The last thing I needed was for the body to be found in public and taken to the Queen's Coroner. It could have been the end of me. It is lucky for you no questions have been asked. But as for Harry here—'

'I'm your faithful servant!' stammered Harry, struggling to his knees.

'Then how did three spies come to follow you tonight? Did you show them a coin too? Who are they, Stubbs? Are they the Queen's men?'

There was silence. I held my breath. If Harry Stubbs told Sir Edward who I was then the Mint Warden would surely know something strange was afoot, and fear that the game was up. He would make his escape straight away. But if Harry *did* tell, then surely he would fear for his own life – for unwittingly leading a Maid of Honour from the Queen's Court to Sir Edward's house.

At last Harry spoke. 'They are beggars, my lord,' he croaked. 'They know nothing. They just chanced to be here tonight.'

I took a deep breath.

'Let me show my loyalty to you,' Harry

pleaded. 'You'll still be wanting a waterman, won't you, my lord?'

'Indeed you are right, Stubbs,' said Sir Edward pleasantly. 'I shall be in want of a waterman . . . for you will be dead!'

'No, my lord, please,' whimpered Harry, trying to grab at Sir Edward's legs with his bound hands.

Sir Edward pushed him away and turned to his henchman. 'Dispose of this pathetic wretch,' he ordered. 'For dead men tell no tales. And I believe that cupboard upstairs is infested with vermin. You might as well get rid of them as well. We can take no chances. A quick slit of the throat will do it.'

I heard Ellie stifle a gasp.

Sir Edward went on. 'But listen hard, Tom Tyler. There must be no bodies found anywhere this time.'

We were in terrible danger. Once our prison was discovered to be empty, Tom Tyler would be looking for us.

Sir Edward strode to the door and flung it open. His page was standing guard outside.

'Stay here,' he told him. 'I am going to the Tower. If anyone asks, your master has been in his bed there all night. Understand?'

The page nodded and Sir Edward disappeared into the darkness. Tom dragged Harry off to the back of the house and we didn't wait to hear any more.

'We must get out of here!' I said. 'Now. Before the bodyguard starts looking for us.'

'We can't go out by the door,' whispered Ellie. 'It's guarded. And I believe it's that very same thieving page I caught trying to steal the chalice. I told you he was a wrong 'un. Just wait until I get me hands on 'im.'

'Hush, Ellie!' hissed Masou, coming back into the hall. 'We must be away. There is a window in the next chamber. It is not guarded and there's only a very short drop to the ground. Make haste.'

Ellie and I did not need telling twice. Somewhere in the back of the house was Tom Tyler, and he had dire plans for us.

We scrambled through the window and jumped to the ground. We knew there was no time to strap our skates on and make our escape along the river, so we kept to the Strand, and ran as fast as we could.

After a few moments we stopped to catch our breath. There was no sound of pursuit.

'We must get to Whitehall,' I panted. 'We have to tell the Queen everything. Sooner or later, Tom Tyler will find we have gone. And he might tell Sir Edward.'

'Mr Hatton and the guards must get to the Tower before Sir Edward hops it!' agreed Ellie.

But she looked cold and tired and I wondered if she would make it home. I felt dreadful, for we had just heard a bell strike one of the clock and she would need to be up in a few hours to work in the laundry, even if she had helped foil a plot against Her Majesty's currency. I gave her a hug.

Ahead of us, the Strand widened and I could just make out the Charing Cross. 'We are nearly at Whitehall,' I said. 'Just past the cross, and we'll be at the Court Gate.'

I took Ellie's hand and we hurried along. As we went I started talking about the whole business, partly to sort it out in my own mind and partly to keep Ellie awake. 'So Sir Edward is not what he seems,' I said. 'But I can't understand why he would need to counterfeit coins. He's the Mint Warden and has high status. And he has the support of Sir Thomas Gresham. I thought him already wealthy for he always dresses in the most extravagant way and has an entourage of servants. And yet his great house in the Strand has nothing in it.'

'Then he is not as rich as he claims,' put in Masou.

'In truth, he would need a very big income to live as he has been doing,' I agreed. 'Perhaps he has used up all his money and needs more. And we now know he is the sort of man who would stop at nothing to get what he wants.'

By now we were back at the Court Gate at Whitehall. There was no time for secret passages. I went straight to the guard.

They drew their swords as we approached. I began to shout at the top of my voice.

'I need to see the Queen. It is most urgent! I must speak to Her Majesty at once.'

One of the guards stepped forwards and took me by the arm.

'Unhand me!' I demanded in my haughtiest voice, struggling to free myself. 'I am Lady Grace Cavendish, Maid of Honour to Her Majesty.'

The guard burst out laughing.

'And I'm the King of Spain!' he sneered, looking at my dirty face and torn and grubby clothes.

The other guard nudged him. 'Er, Bill,' he muttered, out of the corner of his mouth. 'That *is* Lady Grace. I've seen her riding out – though better attired, in general.'

The King of Spain took his hands off me as if he'd been burned. 'I'm sorry, your ladyship, I—'

'Stop blathering and take me to Her Majesty!' I ordered. 'At once.'

'Yes, your ladyship,' he stammered. 'Whatever your ladyship pleases. But these two' – he poked a finger at Ellie and Masou – 'are staying here. I don't know them and it's more than my life's worth to let miscreants near to Her Majesty's person.'

I wanted Ellie and Masou with me but there was no time for argument. 'Just take me to the Queen!' I shouted. I turned to my friends. 'I will have you released as soon as I can.'

My guard then puffed out his chest and led me through the palace, roaring at the top of his voice, 'Make way for Lady Grace! Important business with Her Majesty! Make way for her ladyship!' He would have awoken the dead.

The guards outside the Queen's Chamber stood to attention as we approached. We were stopped in our tracks by a roar. 'What in thunder is going on?'

The Queen was standing in the doorway of her outer chamber. She was magnificent in her brocade bedcoat, with her flaming red hair flowing over her shoulders. But she looked furious. The guard dropped to his knees.

I ran to her and bobbed a quick curtsy. 'Your Majesty, I must see you without delay on a matter of State.'

The Queen ran her eyes over my dishevelled state. Then she turned to the guard. 'You are dismissed. Go back to your post.' And she pushed me into her chamber.

As soon as the door closed she turned to me. 'This had better be important, Grace, to bring me from my rest at such an hour – and in such a manner.'

'Indeed it is, Your Majesty!' I exclaimed, before the Queen could start commenting on my appearance. 'I have found out who is behind the counterfeiting.'

The Queen's face lit up at that. 'Out with it then, Grace,' she demanded. 'And he will wish he had never been born.'

I took a deep breath. 'It is your own Mint Warden, Sir Edward Latimer.'

'Nonsense, child,' she said, laughing. 'It is late and you are raving.'

'But it is the truth, Your Majesty,' I insisted. 'I heard it from his own lips. I am afraid he has tricked us all. He is a wolf in sheep's clothing.'

And I told her the whole story.

When I'd finished, the Queen took my hands. 'You have done well, my Lady Pursuivant,' she said gently, 'and put yourself in much danger on my account.'

Then she let go of my hands and strode to the door. 'Fetch Mr Hatton immediately!' she ordered the guard.

I suddenly remembered poor Ellie and Masou, and told the Queen about them.

Her Majesty called the guard back. 'And then release the two honest servants who are detained at the Court Gate,' she told him.

As soon as Mr Hatton appeared, bleary-eyed with sleep, Her Majesty ordered him to take his Gentlemen of the Guard and go to the Tower to arrest Sir Edward Latimer and his conspirators for counterfeiting and murder.

If Mr Hatton was surprised at what he heard and saw, he showed no sign of it, but started to make his preparations.

'Let me go with them, Your Majesty,' I pleaded.

'Certainly not,' snapped the Queen. 'You have been in enough danger for one night.'

'But Your Majesty,' I dared to argue, 'I am the only one who you know can distinguish the real coins from the counterfeit – apart from Sir Thomas Gresham, that is – and surely you will not send him to the arrest of his own protégé.'

The Queen hesitated. 'Very well, Grace, you may go.' She turned to Mr Hatton. 'Lady Grace will accompany you and I charge you with her safety.'

Mr Hatton tried not to look as if he thought that the Queen was mazed. He bowed. 'My lady shall have two of my best men to guard her.'

I was about to protest at that but the expression on Her Majesty's face silenced me.

And then I had hardly time to breathe as we descended to the main courtyard, where horses were being saddled. I had not even had time to change my clothes, but now I had a guard's red cloak around my shoulders. I confess I did have a moment of doubt about going when I thought how I would have to ride all the way – and it would not be a slow trot! But to my relief I was handed up to ride pillion behind one of my bodyguards, and for my safety I was told not to ride side-saddle as I usually did, but to sit astride the horse. My other guard rode close by so I felt quite safe.

It was quite unlike the slow progress we had made with Sir Edward when we had visited the Tower before. The drumming of the horses' hooves in the night brought people to their windows as we passed and I felt very important! Safe in my pocket was a true silver coin. I had asked the Queen to give me one of her six precious new coins so I could prove the others to be counterfeit.

We dismounted a little way from the Bulwark Gate and Mr Hatton gave his men instructions to charge in, being as loud and terrifying as possible, in order that Sir Edward and his men might be scared into giving themselves up.

I had my doubts about this plan, so I ran over to speak to Mr Hatton. 'I know the real Sir Edward,' I said. 'He is not a man to cower in the corner when he hears your guard on their way. May I suggest we take him by surprise? I think that way you will have a better chance of taking your prize back to Her Majesty.'

Mr Hatton nodded. He had a whispered conversation with the yeoman warder at the gate, and then we hurried silently over the moat, and on to the Byward Tower.

Everywhere I went I was flanked by my two shadows. I felt sorry for the Queen, never stepping out without bodyguards.

My bodyguards and I followed Mr Hatton and four of his guard stealthily up the stairs of the Byward Tower towards Sir Edward's rooms.

It was all very quiet. The guards slipped their swords from their sheaths, then Mr Hatton broke down the door of the bedchamber and the guards rushed in.

But the chamber was empty and the bed had not been slept in. There was no sign of any coins, counterfeit or otherwise.

'I think our bird has flown,' muttered Mr Hatton.

I wasn't giving up that easily. Sir Edward

could not have had time to get far. He might have only just escaped. I rushed to one of the windows and looked out over the Thames. Perhaps he had taken a boat.

But there was no sign of any craft leaving the Tower. I went to another window. This looked out over the battlements. Nothing here apart from the gleam of the cannons in the moonlight. There was one more window which gave over Mint Street. I peered eagerly into the darkness through the mullioned glass. Nothing was moving in the shadowy street.

I felt weariness overwhelm me. After all we'd done we, were too late. Then, in one of the buildings on Mint Street, I saw a brief flicker of light. 'There's someone at the mint!' I gasped. 'Sir Edward may yet be there!'

With their swords still drawn, the guards led the way back down the stairs. The whole company crept along Mint Street. Mr Hatton motioned for the guards to check the windows of each workshop as we passed. They shook their heads at every one.

Finally, we came to the gold and silver Press

House. We could see a dim light inside. Mr Hatton held up his hand for us to stop. Then he nodded and the guards burst into the room. I followed with my trusty bodyguards.

Three men were filling sacks with silver coins. There were trussels and piles and clipping shears strewn over the workbenches.

The men looked up, aghast, as we entered and I recognized them as labourers from my visit to the mint. The guards wasted no time. They rushed forward and took them, two to a man, holding them fast.

At this moment, the door to the Melting House opened and Sir Edward Latimer strode in.

Seeing us, he became in a trice the dainty Sir Edward we had seen at Court. He threw his hands up in horror. 'What is going on?' he exclaimed. 'Why are you here, Mr Hatton?'

'I am to take you and your accomplices before the Queen to answer charges of counterfeiting and murder,' said Mr Hatton grimly.

Sir Edward could have taken his place with any band of players, for he acted the innocent to perfection. 'Counterfeit?' he gasped, clutching his hands to his chest. 'I do not understand. My men are merely struggling to fulfil the Queen's orders for her new coin.' He picked up a metal pile with the Queen's likeness engraved on it and held it out to us. 'We are burning the midnight oil, as you can see. And as for murder—'

'These are not Her Majesty's true coins,' I said, stepping forward into the light. 'And I can prove it.'

Sir Edward laughed lightly. 'Lady Grace? What an honour that you should visit the mint again – but at such an hour? Now, come, Hatton, release these good men so that they may get on with their work and we'll sup some ale together.'

I snatched a coin from one of the sacks and held it next to the one the Queen had given me. 'Your men are making false coins,' I declared. 'See, they have alloy in them and are duller than the true silver one.'

Mr Hatton stepped forward to peer at the coins. I could tell he had seen the difference between them, and the truth of my words, for his mouth tightened and he whirled back to face Sir Edward. I waited for Sir Edward to admit all, but he spun round to berate his labourers. 'You base wretches!' he shouted. 'What villainy is this? Counterfeiting? Murder? Take them away, Mr Hatton. They deserve no mercy.'

'But you said—' one of his labourers began.

'Silence, you varlet!' thundered Sir Edward. 'Now, Mr Hatton, I will certainly go and explain all to the Queen on the morrow. I am mortified that this should have been going on beneath my very nose.'

Mr Hatton hesitated. Surely he would not disobey the orders of the Queen? But I believe at that moment he was taken in by Sir Edward.

My thoughts were racing. I had to get the villain to admit his guilt. I was certain that if he was not arrested immediately he would be far away by dawn. Then I remembered the house on the Strand. 'You have a fine residence by Somerset House, do you not, Sir Edward?' I asked, trying to sound as sweet as Lady Sarah.

'Indeed, my lady,' he answered gallantly. 'And I would be honoured by a visit from you at any time.'

'Thank you, sir,' I said, giving a pretty curtsy. '*Now* would be an excellent time. I am particularly interested in the chamber on the second floor, for I am told it contains your store of counterfeit coins.' I saw Sir Edward's face blanch. 'And we could ask Tom Tyler where he has put Harry Stubbs's body – having killed him on your foul orders.'

The mask fell from Sir Edward's face. With a snarl, he leaped forward, and before I knew what had happened he had me in an arm lock and was holding the pile with its spike pressed to my throat. I thought my heart would stop, it was beating so hard in my chest.

My bodyguards stepped towards us to free me.

'Nobody move!' Sir Edward hissed, pulling me roughly towards the open door. 'I will have safe passage or I will spill the life's blood of this meddling maid.'

The men hesitated and drew back, seeing that Sir Edward meant what he said.

I could hardly keep my wits, but I knew I had to if I were to save my life. I did not believe Sir Edward would let me live even if he did escape.

'Surely you know that this cannot work, Sir Edward,' I said through clenched teeth. 'Mr Hatton will at any minute order his men to attack, whether or not my life is in danger.'

'Quiet!' spat my captor.

'Why not give yourself up like a true man,' I persisted, 'and face the consequences?'

Sir Edward struck me hard on the side of the face with the pile. 'I told you to keep silent!' he growled. My cheek throbbed with pain and I bit my lip so as not to give him the satisfaction of hearing me cry out.

I had to think fast. What would Masou do? He would wriggle out of this somehow. Trickery! That was it – but what trickery could I use? I clenched my fists in desperation – and felt my fingers tighten around the two coins. And that gave me an idea.

We were in the open doorway of the Press House now. Without moving my arm, I flicked the coins behind me and out onto the cobbles of Mint Street. They made a wonderful loud chinking noise and Sir Edward instinctively turned his head to see who was behind him. Taken off guard, he loosened his grip and I sank my teeth into the hand that held the pile.

Sir Edward let out a terrible oath and dropped his makeshift weapon. In an instant one of my bodyguards had pulled me to safety within the Press House, and the Queen's Guards were upon Sir Edward.

The rest of it passed in a blur. One of my bodyguards told me afterwards that I looked close to fainting as I was rescued. What nonsense! It was just that everything happened so quickly, I wasn't sure what was going on.

Amongst the uproar, I heard a scuffle and a terrified yelp from Sir Edward and I think someone must have tried to run him through, for I heard Mr Hatton declare, 'Stay your swords. He must be taken alive. He will answer to the Queen for his villainy.'

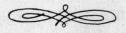

Still in the Queen's own chamber, some time later

I stopped just now and put down my quill. The Queen came to me directly and wouldn't listen when I tried to tell her I just had writer's cramp and needed to stretch my fingers. She threatened to call for my Uncle Cavendish, but I finally managed to persuade her that all was well. I didn't want to submit to his ministrations again. It was bad enough when we returned from the Tower.

I had only suffered a tiny nick in the skin, but you would have thought I'd nearly had my head chopped off for all the fuss. I was carried to the Queen's Chamber on her orders – though I was perfectly able to walk by then – and my uncle sent for.

Her Majesty paced up and down. 'Incompetent bodyguards,' she muttered. 'How I shall deal with them and their master

– allowing you to be put in such danger!'

It took all my skill to persuade her that it was not their fault, for Sir Edward was a very cunning character and had fooled us all.

My uncle looked more bleary-eyed than usual, for it must have been about five of the clock, and he would have been counting on a few more hours' sleep before he had to face the day. He stumbled in, spent many minutes poring over my horoscope, and then proceeded to bleed me to balance my humours. I am sure I shouldn't say this, but I don't know why he bothered with the horoscope, for I think he would have bled me anyway.

'What do you expect, Grace?' he muttered out of the Queen's hearing. He sounded half cross and half worried. 'Chasing about at night and confronting dangerous men! It is small wonder that your humours needed balancing. Now turn this way!'

He inspected my bruised cheek (which looked very colourful in the Queen's looking glass but was hardly hurting at all) and tied a poultice of egg yolk, oil of roses and turpentine in a bandage round my head. Then he gave me an infusion of willow bark to drink. And I slept deeply in Her Majesty's own bed until just before noon.

I awoke to find the Queen gone and Mrs Champernowne tutting and bustling over me. I knew she was desperate to hear of my adventures and eager to scold me for them, too, but I know it was mostly because she was worried about me, so I tried to assure her that I was well.

She insisted I ate some broth, and helped me to dress in my second best gown and stomacher and laced the sleeves on herself. Then she took me to the Queen's Privy Chamber. On the way I pulled off my poultice and threw it into a corner. I wasn't going to look like a mad girl with the toothache.

Unusually the Chamber was not seething with people. There was just Her Majesty, Mr Hatton, Secretary Cecil and Sir Thomas Gresham, and everyone was looking very grave. We curtsied low as we entered, then I was led to a seat of honour by Her Majesty's side and

Mrs Champernowne bustled away, probably to calm her agitation by fussing over the other Maids of Honour.

'Gentlemen,' said the Queen, in a low voice, 'I need hardly tell you that what passes between us in this chamber must be kept most secret.'

The three gentlemen bowed solemnly.

I had a sudden moment of panic. No one here knew that I was the Queen's Lady Pursuivant. Would the Queen be able to explain away my involvement in the night's events, or would all here present learn the truth? In which case, I could no longer be Her Majesty's secret Lady Pursuivant!

I need not have worried.

'You are all privy to the dire knowledge that my new coin has been counterfeited,' she said. 'Lady Grace Cavendish is here on my express orders as it was her sharp eyes that first discovered it. On the instant that I heard word of this treachery I dispatched spies to find out the truth and bring the miscreants to justice. This they have done, and they have my eternal gratitude for it.' She looked at me as she said this. Then she turned to the guards at the door. 'Now bring the ringleader before me.'

Sir Edward Latimer, pale and dishevelled, was dragged in by two guards and pushed to his knees in front of the Queen. His hands were tightly bound in front of him. Sir Thomas Gresham started as he saw his protégé and Mr Cecil put a hand on his arm.

'What have you to say for yourself, Sir Edward?' barked Her Majesty. 'You were wont to make us a very pretty picture of the gallant knight, yet I see you are nought but a black-hearted villain!'

Sir Edward kept his lips tightly together and stared at the floor. I was rather pleased to see his bitten hand was now a dull purple. I hoped it still hurt.

'Have you nothing to say?' demanded the Queen. 'Or are you saving it all for your trial for counterfeiting and murder, not to mention the attempted abduction of my Maid of Honour.'

Sir Edward kept his silence.

'Very well.' The Queen was icy. 'Then Mr

Hatton will tell us of your misdeeds. Your devoted labourers were most willing to divulge all to him.'

I shivered. I could imagine the labourers had taken one look at the torturers' thumb-screws, deep in the bowels of the White Tower, and told all they knew.

'If it please Your Majesty, it transpires that Latimer's young pages are nothing but common thieves, and have been stealing silver all over London to use for the counterfeit coins,' Mr Hatton explained.

So Ellie had been right. Sir Edward's page had been about to steal the silver chalice from the Great Hall. And I suddenly remembered that Lady Sarah's uncle had been robbed of his silver – perchance he had been victim of the same criminals. Lady Sarah would not be pleased to find that Sir Edward had been responsible for the robbery, and thus her lack of a new gown.

'At night, when the mint was supposed to be closed down,' Mr Hatton went on, 'Latimer and his accomplices would take their stolen silver, melt it down with tin to make an alloy and use the very dies designed for Her Majesty's new coin to strike their miserable copies. The Yeomen Guard were told this was all for the Queen and must be kept secret.'

'But what of Master Petty?' I exclaimed. 'Did he not question the night-time workings of the mint? Sir Edward told us that he is the Master Moneyer, so surely he would have known that extra minting was going on. He seemed an honest man.'

Sir Edward raised his head and stared at me. 'He is,' he said sourly. 'So I had to be sure that my men were last to finish at night and first to start in the morning to allay suspicion. And Master Petty has found himself sleeping very well these past few weeks, with a little tincture of poppy in his evening ale.'

Now I knew why Master Petty seemed so strangely tired when we met him at the mint!

'What has happened to all these counterfeit coins?' asked Secretary Cecil gravely.

The Queen looked at me and nodded.

'Sir Edward has been lowering the coins

from a window at the Tower to a boatman in his employ,' I explained. 'This boatman, Harry Stubbs, has been taking them to Sir Edward's house in the Strand, where they have been stored, ready for him to use when Her Majesty's new coin is circulated. The body we found on the ice was Harry Stubbs's brother, Will. He found out about the counterfeiting and was murdered on Sir Edward's orders.' Everyone looked at me. They must have been wondering how I could possibly know this. 'Or so I have been told,' I added hurriedly.

'But Edward, why?' burst out Sir Thomas Gresham. 'You had my support and a good standing at Court. Her Majesty's Mint Warden is a most prestigious position. Could you not have been satisfied?'

'That was never enough!' spat Sir Edward. 'I wanted a fine house and fine clothes and the esteem that comes with them. And it was all within my grasp.' He seemed to have forgotten the Queen's presence as the poisonous words slipped from his lips. He looked wild, as if he had escaped from the Bedlam asylum.

'It wouldn't have been long before a wealthy Maid of Honour or Queen's Lady would have been mine to marry. But until then, maintaining my status and appearance required more money than I had. So I devised a clever plan to meet my expenses – no one ever needed to know. But thanks to the fools I employed, the secret was let out and now I shall die for their stupidity.'

'Your words demean you, sir,' said the Queen coldly. 'Your actions are unforgivable. You would have debased my coin and ruined our fine standing in Europe in one fell swoop. That is treachery in my eyes. And you have made two wives into widows. Murder and treachery carry a heavy penalty.'

She motioned to the guards. 'Take this base wretch from my sight,' she commanded.

And Sir Edward Latimer was led away. It was strange to think he would likely be going back to the Tower which he knew so well – although I doubt he was familiar with the chamber he would now be housed in.

Sir Thomas Gresham fell to his knees in

front of the Queen. He looked heartsick and I felt most sorry for him. 'Pray forgive me, My Liege,' he said in broken tones. 'For I unwittingly put this viper amongst us.'

'To your feet, Sir Thomas,' said the Queen kindly, extending her hand for him to kiss. 'I know you to be a loyal and faithful servant. We have worked hard together in the past to make our currency good and true.'

'Then let us make haste to distribute your new coin without delay,' said Sir Thomas eagerly.

The Queen shook her head. 'I have done with this coin,' she said. 'It has brought nothing but misery. I would that you give orders for all the existing griffin coins, counterfeit and genuine, to be melted down forthwith. And we will not speak of it further.'

I was relieved to hear this. The Queen's griffins have caused me to be out in the cold night air, imprisoned and almost killed. But worse than that, the Queen has been in a foul temper throughout, which makes everyone's life a misery!

Her Majesty then insisted I rest further after

my ordeal and ordered me back to her chamber. She would have had me back to bed, but I begged to be allowed to sit up, and that is when I was tucked into this chair and under the mink.

As I sit here and write I still find it hard to credit that Sir Edward 'Dainty Ways' Latimer was behind the counterfeiting and murders. But a good Lady Pursuivant must keep it in mind that villains come in all shapes and demeanours.

And now I am almost dying from the heat of this cloak and must tactfully find an excuse to be rid of it. Perhaps I should urgently need the privy, which would not be surprising after all the possets Her Majesty has kindly forced down my throat.

Late evening – in my chamber, after impromptu revels

Lady Sarah is most put out. She refuses to speak to me, so the air in our chamber is not only cold on account of the dampened fire, but also frosty on account of my lady's grumpy mood. But I mustn't run ahead of myself.

The Queen was finally convinced that I could be freed, and Mrs Champernowne brought me back to my chamber. Word must have got round, for on the way, Ladies and Gentlemen of the Court stopped to gawp at my bruise and to admire my courage. I will be the talk of Whitehall until a new diversion occurs. I hope it is soon. If I were Lady Jane I would be making the most of it, but in truth I was beginning to tire of my fame by the time we reached my bedchamber. And I would have people forget it, for I may be needed as Lady Pursuivant again and I wish to appear as an ordinary Maid of Honour.

Once back in my chamber, I had to endure endless questions from Lady Sarah about what I had been doing. (She was still talking to me then.) Mary Shelton guessed I could say little of whatever I had been up to, and kindly distracted Sarah as we made ourselves ready for the evening revels.

I think I would have had a tantrum like one

of the Queen's if I had been put to bed early, for Mr Will Somers had announced that to raise Her Majesty's spirits there would be an impromptu acrobatic display – with fire-eating besides – and the kitchens were ordered to prepare a fine feast. I was looking forward to seeing Masou and hoped he'd had enough rest.

Tomorrow I will make an excuse and visit Ellie. I will repay her three times the money she spent on the leaky boat and I will bid her hide it well. And I will make sure that the coins I give her are good and true!

Hell's teeth! Lady Sarah has just stamped past me, jogging my elbow. Now I will have to write round the wiggly line that my quill has produced. But no matter – I have long given up any idea of keeping this daybooke neat as I first intended.

As usual, Mary Shelton and I were ready and waiting while Lady Sarah deliberated between silk sleeves with French lace and ones embroidered with lilies.

Mrs Champernowne put her head round

our door. She was out of breath. 'Girls!' she panted. 'Come quickly, look you. The Queen . . . is calling for you all . . . to process with her . . . into the Great Hall and she will brook no delay.' She stopped to wipe her brow. 'Hurry now, Grace, no dilly dallying!'

I would have liked to remind her that I was actually ready and it was Lady Sarah who deserved her reprimand, but no one kept the Queen waiting. And poor Lady Sarah picked up her sleeves in such a rush that she ended up wearing one of each!

The Queen was waiting for us, surrounded as always by Ladies and Gentlemen of the Court. 'Lady Grace Cavendish!' she said, and she did not sound pleased. I wondered what in Heaven I had done. I had solved her mystery – and within the days she had given me, if only by the skin of my teeth!

'I would have words with you,' she went on. 'Come walk with me.' And she took my arm and pulled me away from the others until we were out of earshot. 'Your kirtle last night was a disgrace! It was ill-fitting and you looked as if you had been in the bear pit.'

I didn't know how to reply. Her Majesty knew exactly what I had been up to, so why was she astonished about my clothes? In fact it was a surprise that my kirtle had ended up in one piece! Then I looked at her face and found there was a twinkle in her eye.

'Dear Grace,' she said, laughing and taking my hand, 'tomorrow you will be fitted for a new gown and I will insist that the bodice and sleeves are decorated with ruby and diamond brooches!' Then she added in a much lower voice, 'I am very grateful to my Lady Pursuivant. Your dear mother, God rest her soul, would have been so proud. Yet I pray I will not have to call upon you again too soon.'

'I am ever at your service, Your Majesty,' I promised, 'for now I have the taste for traitors!' And I bared my teeth like a dog.

The Queen threw her head back and laughed heartily and I felt a warm glow of happiness.

Lady Sarah has scattered her clothes all about,

pulled on her nightgown and flounced into bed without even a goodnight. She does not like the attention I have had today, but most of all, she has found out that I am to have a new gown when she is not. She says she will never speak to me again.

I think I shall survive.

GLOSSARY

apothecary – an Elizabethan chemist

Bedlam – the major asylum for the insane in London during Elizabethan times – the name came from Bethlem Hospital

blank – a rough square of metal, ready to be turned into a coin

bleeding – when a vein is opened to allow blood to flow out of the body. This was actually thought to be beneficial to one's health in Elizabethan times!

bodice – the top part of a woman's dress

Bridewell – a famous London prison

bumroll – a sausage-shaped piece of padding worn round the hips to make them look bigger

copper – usually a copper saucepan or cauldron used for cooking

cups; in one's cups – drunk, intoxicated by alcohol

daybooke – a book in which you would record your sins each day so that you could pray about them. The idea of keeping a diary or journal grew out of this. Grace is using hers as a journal *die* – a coining tool bearing the design of one side of a coin. This tool would be carefully positioned over a 'blank' (see above) and then struck hard so that its design would be pressed into the metal blank. Two dies would be needed for one coin – one for each side.

duds – clothing

flagon – a large jug-like vessel often used for holding wine

flax-wench – an insulting term for a woman

gunwale – the upper edge of a boat's side

halberd – a weapon consisting of a battle-axe and pike mounted on a long handle

heresy – a religious opinion contradicting the established views of the church

hose – tight-fitting cloth trousers worn by men

humours – the fluids of the body which were thought to control health and temperament

Inns of Court – collective name for the four buildings in London where originally schools of law were held

jerkin – a close-fitting, hip-length, usually sleeveless jacket *kirtle* – the skirt section of an Elizabethan dress

Lady-in-Waiting – one of the ladies who helped to look after the Queen and kept her company

litter; littermen – a covered and curtained seat for carrying passengers, supported on long wooden poles; the men who carried the litter through the streets

Maid of Honour – a younger girl who helped to look after the Queen like a Lady-in-Waiting

manchet rolls – whole white bread

Mary Shelton – one of Queen Elizabeth's Maids of Honour (a Maid of Honour of this name really did exist, see below). Most Maids of Honour were not officially 'ladies' (like Lady Grace) but they had to be of born of gentry

masque – a masquerade, a masked ball

mead – an alcoholic drink made with honey

Miss Wiseacre – title jokingly given to one who pretends to great knowledge or cleverness

moneyer – an authorized coin-maker

mullioned glass – small pieces of glass held together by strips of lead to form a window *palliasse* – a thin mattress

penner – a small leather case which could be attached to a belt. It was used for holding quills, ink, knife and any other equipment needed for writing

pike, pikestaff – a spear-like weapon

pile – one of the dies (see above), the one bearing the Queen's image

pillion seat – a saddle for a woman which included a soft cushion

poppy tincture – a medicine for inducing sleep

posset – a hot drink made from sweetened and spiced milk curdled with ale or wine

Presence Chamber – the room where Queen Elizabeth would receive people

Privy Gallery – a gallery in Whitehall Palace

Privy Garden – Queen Elizabeth's private garden

pursuivant – one who pursues someone else

Queen's Guard – these were more commonly known as the Gentlemen Pensioners – young noblemen who guarded the Queen from physical attacks

Secretary Cecil – William Cecil, an administrator for the Queen (was later made Lord Burghley)

Shaitan – the Islamic word for Satan, though it means a trickster and a liar rather than the ultimate evil

stanchion – a supporting post or beam

stomacher – a heavily embroidered or jewelled piece for the centre front of a bodice

sweetmeats – sweets

thumbscrew – an instrument of torture for compressing the thumb

Tilting Yard – area where knights in armour would joust or 'tilt' (i.e. ride at each other on horseback with lances)

tinder box – small box containing some quick-burning tinder, a piece of flint, a piece of steel and a candle for making fire and thus light

tiring woman – a woman who helped a lady to dress

toothcloth – a coarse cloth, often beautifully embroidered, used for rubbing teeth clean

trencher – a wooden platter

truckle bed – a small bed on wheels stored under the main bed *trussel* – one of the dies (see above), the one bearing the design for the back of the coin

tumbler – acrobat

ware bench – bench on which items for sale could be displayed

waterman – a man who rowed a ferry boat on the Thames – a kind of Elizabethan cab driver

White Tower – oldest part of the Tower of London

willow-bark infusion – a drink made of willow bark, which was used as a painkiller. It was later developed into aspirin

Withdrawing Chamber – the Queen's private rooms

In 1485, Queen Elizabeth I's grandfather, Henry Tudor, won the battle of Bosworth Field against Richard III and took the throne of England. He was known as Henry VII. He had two sons, Arthur and Henry. Arthur died while still a boy, so when Henry VII died in 1509, Elizabeth's father came to the throne and England got an eighth king called Henry – the notorious one who had six wives.

Wife number one – Catherine of Aragon – gave Henry one daughter called Mary (who was brought up as a Catholic), but no living sons. To Henry VIII this was a disaster, because nobody believed a queen could ever govern England. He needed a male heir.

Henry wanted to divorce Catherine so he could marry his pregnant mistress, Anne Boleyn. The Pope, the head of the Catholic Church, wouldn't allow him to annul his marriage, so Henry broke with the Catholic Church and set up the Protestant Church of

England – or the Episcopal Church, as it's known in the USA.

Wife number two – Anne Boleyn – gave Henry another daughter, Elizabeth (who was brought up as a Protestant). When Anne then miscarried a baby boy, Henry decided he'd better get somebody new, so he accused Anne of infidelity and had her executed.

Wife number three – Jane Seymour – gave Henry a son called Edward, and died of childbed fever a couple of weeks later.

Wife number four – Anne of Cleves – had no children. It was a diplomatic marriage and Henry didn't fancy her, so she agreed to a divorce (wouldn't you?).

Wife number five – Catherine Howard – had no children either. Like Anne Boleyn, she was accused of infidelity and executed.

Wife number six – Catherine Parr – also had no children. She did manage to outlive Henry, though, but only by the skin of her teeth. Nice guy, eh?

Henry VIII died in 1547, and in accordance with the rules of primogeniture (whereby the first-born son inherits from his father), the person who succeeded him was the boy Edward. He became Edward VI. He was strongly Protestant, but died young in 1553.

Next came Catherine of Aragon's daughter, Mary, who became Mary I, known as Bloody Mary. She was strongly Catholic, married Philip II of Spain in a diplomatic match, but died childless five years later. She also burned a lot of Protestants for the good of their souls.

Finally, in 1558, Elizabeth came to the throne. She reigned until her death in 1603. She played the marriage game – that is, she kept a lot of important and influential men hanging on in hopes of marrying her – for a long time. At one time it looked as if she would marry her favourite, Robert Dudley, Earl of Leicester. She didn't though, and I think she probably never intended to get married – would you, if you'd had a dad like hers? So she never had any children.

She was an extraordinary and brilliant woman, and during her reign, England first started to become important as a world power. Sir Francis Drake sailed round the world – raiding the Spanish colonies of South America for loot as he went. And one of Elizabeth's favourite courtiers, Sir Walter Raleigh, tried to plant the first English colony in North America – at the site of Roanoke in 1585. It failed, but the idea stuck.

The Spanish King Philip II tried to conquer England in 1588. He sent a huge fleet of 150 ships, known as the Invincible Armada, to do it. It failed miserably – defeated by Drake at the head of the English fleet – and most of the ships were wrecked trying to sail home. There were many other great Elizabethans, too – including William Shakespeare and Christopher Marlowe.

After her death, Elizabeth was succeeded by James VI of Scotland, who became James I of England and Scotland. He was almost the last eligible person available! He was the son of Mary Queen of Scots, who was Elizabeth's cousin, via Henry VIII's sister.

His son was Charles I – the King who was beheaded after losing the English Civil War.

The stories about Lady Grace Cavendish are set in the year 1569, when Elizabeth was thirty-six and still playing the marriage game for all she was worth. The Ladies-in-Waiting and Maids of Honour at her Court weren't servants – they were companions and friends, supplied from upper-class families. Not all of them were officially 'ladies' – only those with titled husbands or fathers; in fact, many of them were unmarried younger daughters sent to Court to find themselves a nice rich lord to marry.

All the Lady Grace Mysteries are invented, but some of the characters in the stories are real people – Queen Elizabeth herself, of course, and Mrs Champernowne and Mary Shelton as well. There never was a Lady Grace Cavendish (as far as we know!) – but there were plenty of girls like her at Elizabeth's Court. The real Mary Shelton foolishly made fun of the Queen herself on one occasion – and got slapped in the face by Elizabeth for her trouble! But most of the time, the Queen seems to have been protective and kind to her Maids of Honour. She was very strict about boyfriends, though. There was one simple rule for boyfriends in those days: you couldn't have one. No boyfriends at all. You would get married to a person your parents chose for you and that was that. Of course, the girls often had other ideas!

Later on in her reign, the Queen had a full-scale secret service run by her great spymaster, Sir Francis Walsingham. His men, who hunted down priests and assassins, were called 'pursuivants'. There are also tantalizing hints that Elizabeth may have had her own personal sources of information – she certainly was very well informed, even when her counsellors tried to keep her in the dark. And who knows whom she might have recruited to find things out for her? There may even have been a Lady Grace Cavendish, after all!

A note on the Tower of London

The Tower was officially one of the royal palaces, but Queen Elizabeth I did not like it, which was hardly surprising since she had been a prisoner there during her sister Mary's reign. Her mother, Anne Boleyn, had also been beheaded there.

However, the Tower had many functions, besides being a palace and the Royal Mint. It was also a prison, and the Queen often threw her enemies into the Tower. In fact, it was teeming with subjects who had plotted against her and the torturers were kept very busy. Her Majesty's torturers worked in the dungeons of the White Tower, which was the oldest part of the Tower of London and said to have been built using mortar mixed with blood!

Not all prisoners were tortured. Many spent their time languishing in one of the towers with very little to do. And a few of them left their mark. Visitors today can see ancient graffiti on the walls of the Beauchamp Tower. It is even said that Elizabeth I herself scratched some words into the stone when she was a prisoner – the Tudor equivalent of 'Lizzie woz 'ere'!

We might think of the Tower as a place of

execution, but most beheadings actually took place outside the ramparts on Tower Hill, for all to watch – usually thousands of unruly Londoners. Only the lucky few got a private execution *inside* the walls on Tower Green.

But aside from its more grisly functions, the Tower also housed an immense armoury, where weapons and armour were crafted. The Crown Jewels were kept in the Jewel House. And there were even two taverns for the thirsty workers. From the thirteenth century onwards, animals were kept in a menagerie in the Lion Tower. At one time there was even an elephant – though it didn't live long. Visitors in Queen Elizabeth I's time would have been more likely to see a couple of scrawny lions and a tiger, in tiny cages – sadly there was no RSPCA in those days. In the nineteenth century the menagerie was moved to Regent's Park and became London Zoo.